G R JORDAN

Vengeance is Mine

Highlands & Islands Detective Thrillers #28

Vengeance is the act of turning anger in on yourself. On the surface it may be directed at someone else, but it is a surefire recipe for arresting emotional recovery.

JANE GOLDMAN

Contents

Foreword

The events of this book, while based around real locations in the north of Scotland, are entirely fictional and all characters do not represent any living or deceased person. All companies are fictitious representations.

Acknowledgement

To Ken, Jean, Colin, Evelyn, John and Rosemary for your work in bringing this novel to completion, your time and effort is deeply appreciated.

Novels by G R Jordan

The Highlands and Islands Detective series (Crime)

1. Water's Edge
2. The Bothy
3. The Horror Weekend
4. The Small Ferry
5. Dead at Third Man
6. The Pirate Club
7. A Personal Agenda
8. A Just Punishment
9. The Numerous Deaths of Santa Claus
10. Our Gated Community
11. The Satchel
12. Culhwch Alpha
13. Fair Market Value
14. The Coach Bomber
15. The Culling at Singing Sands
16. Where Justice Fails
17. The Cortado Club
18. Cleared to Die
19. Man Overboard!
20. Antisocial Behaviour
21. Rogues' Gallery
22. The Death of Macleod - Inferno Book 1

Kirsten Stewart Thrillers (Thriller)

Jac Moonshine Thrillers

The Contessa Munroe Mysteries (Cozy Mystery)

1. Corpse Reviver
2. Frostbite
3. Cobra's Fang

The Patrick Smythe Series (Crime)

1. The Disappearance of Russell Hadleigh
2. The Graves of Calgary Bay
3. The Fairy Pools Gathering

Austerley & Kirkgordon Series (Fantasy)

1. Crescendo!
2. The Darkness at Dillingham
3. Dagon's Revenge
4. Ship of Doom

Supernatural and Elder Threat Assessment Agency (SETAA) Series (Fantasy)

1. Scarlett O'Meara: Beastmaster

Chapter 01

Eamon Banner could feel the sweat running down the side of his face, but was unsure of what was causing it. It could've been from the exertion, walking up the long road towards the Falls of Shin carpark, located just outside the visitor centre. The slope was significant, and after all, Eamon was a desk man, no fitness guru. He'd rather have gone for a Sunday lunch than a Sunday walk.

It could have been because of the envelope he was holding in his hands. Inside were things that only certain people should know. He had procured them, and though he hadn't looked at them in any detail, he knew what the value of the envelope was. He knew what the cost of it being discovered that he was acquiring it for someone else was as well. Eamon's work, while not the most secretive in the land, was still bound by the Official Secrets Act. A code of silence amongst the people he worked with, and he'd sold out.

But it also could've been the woman he'd sold out to that was causing the sweat. She'd approached him first, although he had spotted her sitting across from him in the café.

Her legs had been bare, although they were so smooth you would've thought she was wearing tights. Her stilettoes

1

weren't high, but the skirt was. You could clearly see her thighs and as for the little top she had on. Resting back in the sunshine, hair flowing out behind her ears, she'd gave him a view he'd failed to pull away from. When she flashed a smile at him, his heart had jumped.

Sandra had walked out. Sandra had taken everything. Eamon hadn't been happy at that, for he thought he'd given Sandra the best years of his life. He thought he'd worked hard for her. Yes, they weren't the most dynamic couple together, but they'd had holidays where they were happy. They'd had two kids, and he still remembered the joy of holding his firstborn.

But she'd walked. She'd walked, and he'd been faithful. He tried to be a decent husband, but she resented the work. She resented the fact he couldn't talk about it, and eventually things had got so bad she started inventing affairs. He was innocent, yet he couldn't show her because he shouldn't show anyone anything about his work.

Well, he wasn't making that mistake this time. Yes, he'd grabbed something he shouldn't have, but it was going to allow him to take hold of something he truly wanted.

'Anne Marie,' she said, approaching his table. He'd been looking at her, and she'd smiled occasionally, and then she'd simply walked over. She hadn't sat opposite; she'd sat in the seat right beside him. Turned, so that nothing of her was obscured by the table. Her leg had swung across and touched his several times while she was talking to him. She had even caught him not looking at her face, and laughed at it. She seemed to appreciate his enjoyment of her physical form.

Anne Marie had done most of the talking, asking him questions about where he'd come from. When he'd asked her about what she did, she talked about starting out as a model, but being the wrong shape so she'd done a different sort of modelling. He was transfixed as she spoke openly about that, but now she was looking to settle down. Looking for someone to share a life with, and then she'd said it. There were just two of them, out on a limb together. Why didn't he take her to dinner?

He had done so two nights later, and she'd appeared in a shimmering dress. She'd been attentive to him the whole time, constantly ready to engage either in conversation or in a gentle embrace.

When he was with her, he felt the fire. Each time, he felt he was ready to give everything to this woman. Every evening, it ended with him dropping her at the door. The fire in him had flamed even more. By now, it was a raging inferno.

He'd been a little surprised when she'd asked about the items she wanted him to get. She'd said it was because her brother was a photographer and he needed to know where people were going to be so he could shoot them for magazines. It would get him a step ahead.

He had said he would do it, and he realised he would do anything for her. Anne Marie was his world now, every bit of her. He had said that maybe he could take her to dinner and she could come back to his place. Crazily, she'd looked at him, slipped an arm around his back, a hand onto his backside and had said to him that for the first time she didn't want the bedroom. For the first time, she wanted to be out in the wild.

He'd stared at her, intrigued. She detailed about coming up here, to the Falls of Shin. They could make love in front of the waterfall in the middle of the night with the cool air around them. He'd wondered if it would be cool air or icy air, given where it was. She had said they would start in the car, and then when they were ready, they'd make a run down to the falls, absolutely nothing on.

These thoughts were driving Eamon on as he approached the carpark at the Falls of Shin. It was reckless; it was madness; it was fun. He would take what he had never had. Yes, he'd been excited around his wife, especially in those early days, but not like this.

Anne Marie was too good to be true. Anne Marie was everything. Ready to be his woman, to be his, and yet with a drive and enthusiasm and ideas that frankly blew his mind. As he reached the crest of the hill and approached the carpark at the visitor centre, he saw one car and a figure standing beside it. Anne Marie's long black hair was hanging out loosely onto bare shoulders.

She wore a thin strapped top, at least as far as he could make out in the poor light. She opened the car door ever so slightly, and the light from inside illuminated her. He saw a skirt that seemed to have forgotten the other half of it, and her legs ending up in- well, there was a nice touch- walking boots. He didn't blame her. Who in their right mind would walk around here in stilettos?

Eamon got close and Anne Marie stepped forward. She folded herself around him, kissing him on the lips. Then deeper excitement filled the air. Eamon was shaking with anticipation.

'Is that my brother's little envelope?' she asked. 'Why don't you give me that?'

Eamon handed it over without even thinking, enthralled by the woman. She stood there and slipped off the skirt, throwing it inside the car. It had been wet during the day and the night air wasn't cold, if moist. He was sure if they ever got wet, it would soon get cold. Starting up the car would be a good idea.

'Oh, Eamon,' she said. 'I'm going to be a minute.'

'A minute?' he said. 'What do you mean, a minute?' Eamon got worried.

'It's okay. I'll be back in just a second. Just a few women's things I need to take care of.'

Eamon wondered what they could be, but he wasn't going to argue.

'Why don't you get inside the car and get ready for me?' She smiled. 'I mean ready. All of it off. I don't want to see a stitch on you when I get back. Maybe I'll come back without a stitch either.'

Eamon's face beamed. He watched from the window as she disappeared off, mesmerised by her buttocks disappearing into the dark. This was going to be good.

Eamon climbed into the car, closing the door, and the light went out. He leaned forward and pushed the embedded light so it illuminated his actions. He then took off his shirt, throwing it to the floor, before bending down and undoing his shoes. *I better take these socks off*, he thought. Nothing worse than getting caught with nothing on and still being in socks. Bit of a turnoff that.

Eamon removed the socks, then reached for his belt, slipped off his trousers, and lastly removed his underpants. He sat in the car, facing the door, which they had stood just outside of. *How should he sit? How should he present himself?* he thought. *What the hell? Who cared?*

From his position, seeing out of the car was difficult. The bright light inside meant everywhere outside looked even darker than it was. It was about two minutes before he heard footsteps approaching. He had expected that Anne-Marie would be bouncing towards him in excitement herself, but there was a quiet shuffle as somebody approached the car. Maybe she was just preparing something, he thought. Maybe she was bracing herself. After all, he was going to be full throttle tonight. He was going to be all action. He heard the click of the door handle and got ready to—the door opened.

At first, all he could see was grey. Maybe she'd gone off to dress up. Then a figure bent down and in came a mask. It was grey, too. It had a face, human, but very stolid and simply cut. He could see eyes looking through. From behind the mask, however, was no long hair emerging.

'What the hell?'

The person entering the car reached down, grabbed his ankles, and pulled him hard. Eamon slid along the seat but threw his arms out. The man continued to pull hard. Eamon slid again, but he wedged his arm between the two front seats of the car and grabbed hold of the top of the rear seat.

For a moment, he held true, trying to kick his legs. He felt he was getting the upper hand slowly when suddenly the man let go. Eamon went to scramble back, but the man appeared inside again, only this time he had a long, thin piece of metal. He drove it at Eamon, hitting him in the face. Eamon cried out, his head snapping backwards. He suddenly felt woozy.

His ankles were grabbed again, and this time he was pulled clean out of the car. He felt the gravel hit his back and grunted in pain. Somebody kicked him in the side. Then he was flipped over, and his arms pulled together at the wrists, while the figure leaned on top of him, driving a knee into his back. He was bound in that position, and then his legs were grabbed and bound, too.

The figure twisted him over again, bent down, one hand upon his neck, one underneath an arm, pulling him vaguely upright. Then the figure bent, dipping his shoulder into Eamon's mid-rift so that Eamon fell over the top of him in a collapsed L-shape. Hanging onto his legs, the figure rose to his feet and began carrying him towards the Falls of Shin.

'What do you want? What the hell's this? Where is Anne-Marie? What have you done with her?'

The figure remained silent and Eamon could hear the rush of the falls. There had been rain, and the river was in good flow, leading to a generous deluge from the waterfall. In the darkness, it was hard to see. All he could make out was the swish of the man's grey habit beneath him. Eamon was carried down towards the waterfall until they stopped short of it. He was dumped onto his back. Up above him, he could see a noose.

Eamon shook now with terror and fear. He looked up at that rope as it descended. He scanned quickly around him and could see the grey figure now allowing the rope to descend. Eamon felt his bladder go weak, and he urinated. There was no sound from the figure beside him.

Once the rope had come down, the figure secured the noose around Eamon's neck. At first, it didn't pick him up with it, instead choosing to drag him up off onto a small rocky outcrop. The pull rope was at the rear of the tree above it, but the noose was further out towards the river. Eamon realised that if he went off that rocky outcrop by the noose, he would fall before being grabbed by the rope so he would hang over the river.

'I know things. Can tell you things. I have got lots of stuff to give. You don't need to kill me. I don't need to...'

He was slapped around the face. His skin was sore from

being pulled over rock, tree and bramble. Then he felt the cool of the rock as he was dumped on the edge. The view to the river was, on any other day, astounding. Tonight., it was utterly terrifying. Not that he could see it in detail, but he could hear the rush of the water. He could hear the crash of the falling deluge.

'Please. Please, I tell you, I've got plenty of stuff. I work for the government. A government worker. I've got loads of secrets I could tell you. You need to keep me alive. You need to...'

Eamon felt the boot kicking him in the back. As he'd believed, he fell forward, then suddenly caught when the tension of the rope kicked in, swing out across the river, back and forward.

His last view was stunning. Wherever you had visited in the world, this would be right up there. A touch of moonlight came across the river, throwing patches of light and opening up small vistas of rushing water.

Eamon was the unluckiest man in the world in two regards. The first was that the rope had twisted, so he was looking the wrong way for those vistas. But the second, and arguably more important issue, was that the rope had snapped his neck and Eamon Banner was now dead.

Chapter 02

'I'm sure this is only going to be temporary. At the end of the day, Hope, he'll be back. He'll be back, and he'll be running this unit again. I fully expect it. He's just been through such a trauma.'

Hope looked over at the Assistant Chief Constable and tried to gauge his look. Was he truly genuine in his assessment of her friend, Seoras Macleod?

Detective Chief Inspector Seoras Macleod had been tortured and was struggling with the aftereffects of it. The care home had reported that he was having episodes, and although his general health was returning, his mental health was struggling.

'The doctor said to me,' continued Jim, 'that this is pretty normal. His brain's trying to work it out, trying to recover. It's just that he needs space to do that.'

'I'm sure you're right. Whatever comes will come,' said Hope, 'and I'll be there for him, Jim. I'm not worried about that. It's what you're proposing here. I can't step up and be the DCI. I've only just got made up to DI.'

'I'm not wanting you to step in and take the paperwork and that. I just want you to run the unit. There are a couple of other units that come under Seoras' jurisdiction. All you've got to do is to be the listening ear for those. Scan their reports when they come in.'

'We're still in the middle of a major hunt for this man, Jim. We didn't get the ringleader of these grey-masked people, and he's the one we need. He didn't go away last time, Jim.'

'All the more reason I need somebody capable here. Clarissa's back. Clarissa's back with you. That's got to count for something. Cunningham's good. Patterson's going to do desk work. Maybe he'll be ready for the field in a few months. We'll see. You've got Ross. Heck, bump Ross up. Make Ross the number two in the unit.'

'I can't make him number two,' said Hope. 'Can't move him past Clarissa. She's a sergeant.'

'Make him an acting sergeant. The man's at the core of this unit, Seoras always said so.'

'He is.'

Hope turned and looked out the window behind her. Jim had come down to her office with his proposal, so clearly, he was coming with as many olive branches as he could. He hadn't summoned her, and maybe that was meant to look like he wasn't just dumping things on her. They could bring somebody else in, of course. A replacement DCI, but would that mean that temporary could become permanent quickly?

If Seoras came back—no, when Seoras came back—this job needed to be here for him. This is what he did. He was the one she wanted to work with. The team could do with stability as well. They don't want somebody else taking over and shaking things up. Clarissa could walk any minute. Hope felt that she was back as a bandaid for the team. Possibly back because she had unfinished business. Well, they all did. They all felt it was unfinished. They would get this—she shouldn't say the word.

This man, she corrected herself, who did all of this to Seoras.

'Well, what about it?' asked Jim. 'Six months. He's bound to be back by six months.'

Jim was persuasive. Six months was a good time. There was a lot of work on her, though. She was already under a lot of stress.

'You're picking up the basic paperwork, salaries, hours, holiday, all that stuff. All the stuff that Seoras would normally pick up and I don't touch. I'll handle cases and review them. I'll keep going through your other units and make sure they're on the track, but I'm working out of here.'

'Well, that's your choice,' said Jim, 'but Linda's upstairs. She can be very useful.'

'Linda will be very useful for you,' said Hope, smiling, 'because you're doing all that paperwork.'

Jim stood up and shook hands with Hope. He could look her in the eye because he was a reasonably tall man and her six-foot figure didn't dwarf him like it did many of her colleagues.

'You know, one day,' said Jim, 'you'll work without him. One day you'll have a unit. He won't be here. He's got at least twenty years on you, Hope. You can't work with him forever. He wouldn't want you to, anyway. He sees you as the future. You and Ross, not the old Rottweiler out there.'

Hope grinned when he mentioned Clarissa's nickname. Hope was delighted she was back. She'd been missing, and yet she'd been the one who had come out from retirement to find Macleod. Macleod had always said she was a tough nose that Hope could learn from. Clarissa had gone about her business quietly in truth, and not wholly legally, but she'd found Macleod.

Hope walked Jim to the door of her office, and as she opened it to let him out, Clarissa marched into the other office. There was a brand new pair of tartan trews, and Hope wondered if that was a new shawl. Maybe it'd just been cleaned up.

'Jim,' said Clarissa.

'Clarissa,' said Jim. 'Back on the force. Let's keep it by the book.'

Hope could see that Clarissa was aware of the rest of the team in the office watching the conversation. She gave her a rather meek nod and then walked up to bypass Jim closely.

Hope was in earshot as Clarissa said, 'Well, it'll be legal. By the book, maybe not.'

Jim left the office with a slight shake of the head, causing Hope to smile. It was indeed good to have Clarissa back. The telephone rang in the rear of the office, and Hope saw Ross picking up.

'Have you been to see him?' asked Hope, shouting after Clarissa down the office.

'He's still not right,' she said. 'Still getting issues. He's healing up well, though. I'm going to keep popping in to see him. Jane's left the care home, though. She's fine, other than concerned about Seoras.'

'She's gone home on her own?' queried Hope. 'We haven't had that killer yet. I'll get some security arranged. I'll get—'

'She's not gone home,' said Clarissa. 'She's stopping with me and Frank. Jane'll have people about, and I've got a watch on the place, anyway.'

Hope nodded.

'Boss,' shouted Ross from the back of the room. 'Got a call. There's a body up by the Falls of Shin.'

'Okay,' said Hope. 'Any more detail?'

'Hanging butt-naked from a tree.'

12

'Well, that's a bit more suspicious. Okay, start organising. We're off to Shin.'

Hope turned back into her office and gathered her jacket and then other things from her desk.

Macleod would be all right. This was just temporary. She was taking over while he was there. She could run the team. In fact, it ran itself. There were no big shakes in what was going on. She would be fine. No problems whatsoever.

She picked up her phone, called her partner John, advising him she might be late that night.

'Is it to do with the one from before?'

'Only just got the call in,' said Hope. 'Can't say anything about it. Don't know, but if I can get home tonight, I'll be home tonight.'

John had become much more anxious, especially since Macleod's torture. She understood why. The last thing he'd want was for her to go through that, but it wouldn't be as easy to capture her as Seoras. She'd make sure of that.

She fired up a map of the area around Shin. They'd been up that way before. She remembered the auction house and the first time they'd met Clarissa. That was something to note. Would Clarissa be okay going past that place again? She'd been funny about work lately. She'd been funny about a lot of things. Hope was surprised she came back, and thought it was only Macleod that was driving her to do this. Either way, she was glad to have her.

There was a knock on the door.

'Come in.'

Susan Cunningham strode in, dressed in jeans and a t-shirt, and Hope thought it was a mirror image of herself except for the blonde rather than red hair. She'd grown closer to

13

Cunningham through the last while, and she thought the woman would be good. There were edges to be smoothed off, but she thought Susan was settling into being a detective. Macleod had seen the right things in her and not the rumours around the station about her life and just who she was with at what time.

'They found another body,' said Susan.

'Another one?' asked Hope. 'What, was it just not available to them?'

'It was hiding in the bushes. A naked woman on the floor.'

'So, we've got two naked corpses? What the heck was going on at the Falls of Shin?' asked Hope. 'Right, we'd better get up. I take it Jona's on her way.'

'Yes, Ross checked. She is. I'll get the car,' said Susan.

'Wait,' said Hope. 'Close the door.'

'But we need to—'

'I said close the door,' said Hope. 'Ross will be another four or five minutes at least. Clarissa too. It's fine. They're dead. They will not get any more dead.'

Susan nodded, closed the door, and came close to Hope.

'I've just been given the task of looking after about half of the DCI role. I'm going to need you to step up,' said Hope. 'I've got Patterson working in the office. Clarissa's back, which is good, and normally, I would pick up the other side of the role, but I must head the investigation, so I need my two leaders underneath. I would normally put Ross up, but Ross needs to be where we can make the most use of him, and that's organising everything. You want to be investigating like I normally would. I might send you out more on your own or with a constable.'

'Okay,' said Susan, smiling. 'I can do that.'

14

'But you be careful. We've got Seoras in the hospital. We nearly lost Ross last time. Hunted through the woods, he had to throw himself into a river. This guy we're up against—'

'This guy we're up against is happy to kill. He won't hesitate and clearly has a problem with some of the police. High time we give him a taste of his own medicine.'

'You've been talking to Clarissa,' said Hope.

'A little. She's right, though. We need to strike back at him. We need to—'

'The investigation is key. We need to follow things through, chase the evidence, find out who and where he is, and bring him in.'

'Of course,' said Susan.

'Clarissa might work differently at times, but she knows the rules, and she knows what we need to do. By all means, learn from her, but you won't be her,' said Hope. 'It's not the way you are. You'll be at your best when you follow things through and not chase up hunches, not go and—'

'Beat the information out of others?'

'Extract the information in a robust fashion,' said Hope. 'Clarissa operates on the limits, but when she had to operate outside of them, she resigned. She wasn't here. That's come from experience. It's not the formula we follow.'

'Of course,' said Susan. 'Shall I get the car?'

Hope nodded, and as Susan went to open the door, but Ross pushed his way in.

'Just a little information. There's a word written on the body of the woman, on her forehead. Can't make it out. Not sure what language it is. I think it's Gaelic. I can't tell whether it's Irish Gaelic, Scott's Gaelic, or one of the other similar languages. But it's certainly a word that most of our people

15

seem unfamiliar with. Salachair.'

'Might be worth running it past Seoras at some point, then. He speaks his Gaelic well, or at least he did.'

'How do you know he speaks it well?' asked Ross.

'I heard him talking to someone before,' said Hope.

'Did you know what they were saying?'

'No.'

'Well, he could have said anything then, and badly.'

Hope was noticing something in Ross; there was less of a politeness these days. The last few months had changed him.

'Either way. We'll try to stick it past him. Let's get moving,' said Hope, shooing the pair of them out of her office. Once they'd gone, Hope checked again to make sure she had everything before striding through her door.

Don't be too long, Seoras,' she thought. *Don't be too long.*

Chapter 03

Today had been a good day. Macleod had got up, had breakfast at the care home, which had comprised scrambled eggs and bacon. Yes, the coffee was the usual rubbish, except that today Glenda had been on.

Glenda was a middle-aged woman with a big broad smile and bushy brunette hair. Her jolly disposition lent itself to more than just her outlook on life. She had listened to Macleod whinging about the coffee every time she'd poured it. She'd gone out and got him some special coffee along with a cafetiere.

Now, it wasn't perfect if Macleod was being honest. It didn't have that barista touch. The coffee wasn't extracted under pressure. Nor was it carefully handled to produce an excellent latte or cappuccino, but the flavour was there. For simple black coffee, it was divine after the absolute muck he'd been drinking.

Not that coffee was the biggest worry he had. What was bothering him at the moment was—well, everything. The care home for a start. It was here for convalescence. Most of the people in it were at least not gaga, but it didn't have the cut and thrust of being out on the job. Everything was slow-paced. Everything was rest and recuperation.

For a man like Macleod, that didn't come easy. Jane had always said to him when they went on holiday to sit still. Macleod preferred to be up and wandering around buildings, examining and learning the history, unlike Jane who was happier lying on a beach.

He'd lain on the beach with her many times. She made it easier because he wouldn't have been there on his own, but here in the care home, everything was slow-paced. Sit and read a book. Macleod wasn't against books, but he couldn't just sit and read a book all the time. The other problem was that the only time he got excitement it wasn't the kind he wanted.

The torture had been extreme, to say the least, and Seoras tried not to think about it. However, occasionally, he went through it again. The problem was he was having flashbacks to it, flashbacks that felt real. Each time, he could feel the whip cutting in. He could feel the punches.

His body had done well. It was well healed, but there was a mental exhaustion that kept bringing his body back down. Jane had stayed on at the care home for quite a while, and in truth, they'd let her stay on for two weeks beyond what she should have, but now she was gone.

She had to get out. She had to have a life other than being stuck in here looking at him. They'd get back out together. They'd get back to their house at some point, but she needed to be set free from this chicken coop.

He thought of it as a chicken coop. They fed you. They watered you, sometimes let you out to do this. Other times they shut you in. You just had to sit on your eggs and not create a lot of fuss.

Today, however, he was bowling. They'd taken a small group of the residents in the minibus to go bowling at the sports centre down the road. Macleod had never been a bowler. He'd never really been a sportsman at all, but here was a chance to get out and stretch his legs. Anyway, it was only bowling down a mat inside a sports centre.

Of course, the coffee at the sports centre was disappointing, but he indulged himself with a cola instead. For the most part, he was feeling quite happy. He wasn't winning. He hadn't got a clue what he was doing with the bowls, but he was smiling. As Glenda would've said to him, 'You've taken your face for a joy ride.'

Macleod was sitting down now, awaiting his turn, happy in the knowledge they were to be here for at least another hour. Everyone seemed happier just getting out of their surrounds. Now, the care home was pleasant, but that was the thing. It was nice. But it wasn't your own home. It wasn't dynamic. It was just nice.

If it had been a hotel room for a couple of nights, he'd have said, 'Yes, this is fine.' But over time, Macleod had come to loath his room, being trapped there. He also realised he associated the care home with the flashbacks he was having. That didn't help either. He believed the flashbacks would end when he got out. Therefore, being in the care home was an evil to be overcome. Although he was maybe being a little unfair on the staff.

Macleod gave a sigh as he realised he needed the bathroom, and he gave a wave to one man he was playing with, pointing to the toilets at the far end of the hall. Macleod walked out, not quite striding but with a buzz in his step. He opened the bathroom door and stepped inside. It was a compact unit; one toilet, one small sink, a hand dryer. All the usual suspects. He turned and locked the door and then began his business.

'Mary Smith.'

Macleod flinched. 'Who said that?' He was in a toilet cubicle. 'Who?'

'Mary Smith. Mary Smith. Macleod, Mary Smith.'

Mary Smith had been the woman who had been sexually abused on the Isle of Lewis around the time he'd become an officer. McNeil, the chief officer at the time, had brushed it under the carpet, and years later this had set off a killer. Macleod didn't know why the killer was so involved, but he was. Once he got out of this care home, he'd find out.

'Mary Smith. Who is she? Who is she, Macleod? Mary Smith. Admit it. Admit it. Mary Smith.'

The intensity of the voice built up. Macleod could feel himself beginning to sway under the pressure. He felt like his arms were extended. Held; pinned down.

'Mary Smith. Mary Smith.'

'Don't know a Mary Smith,' said Macleod, suddenly. 'I don't know her. Mary Smith. I knew Mairi, not Mary. Don't know Mary. Wasn't me!'

'Mary Smith. Mary Smith,' said the voice continuously. 'Tell me who Mary Smith is. Why did you do it to Mary Smith? Why did you?'

Macleod swooned. His legs went from under him, and he cluttered to the floor inside the bathroom.

'Mary Smith. You'll tell me. You'll tell me, Macleod. Mary Smith.'

There was a knock on the door. 'Seoras,' said a voice. 'Are you okay, Seoras?'

It was Margaret, one of the care home workers.

'Seoras, are you okay?'

'No,' said the Macleod. He could hear a fumbling with the

lock. He heard it click, and the door opened.

'What are you doing down there?' asked Margaret. 'Let's get you up. Come on.'

There were two arms suddenly hauling him back up to his feet. He stood up, looking a little embarrassed.

'Another episode?'

'Yes,' said Macleod.

'Are you okay?'

'I will be,' he said. 'I didn't get to use the bathroom, though. Guess I better use it.'

'Okay,' said Margaret. 'I'll be outside if you need me. Just shout.'

He turned and closed the door. Macleod completed his ablutions, washed his hands, and came back out to find serious faces looking at him. None more so than Billy.

'Billy, it's not important,' said a voice.

'It is. It's your go, Seoras. Your go. We need you to put this one close.'

What on earth? thought Macleod. *I've just collapsed in the bathroom. The man's an idiot.*

Macleod smiled, nodded, and didn't quite stride, but walked with a little unease up to his last bowl. He looked at the far end and someone showed roughly where he should bowl and he threw it down.

'Dammit,' said Billy. 'That was crap.'

'Now, Billy, we're just here to have some fun,' said Margaret.

Billy had been a bowler and was ultra-competitive. Macleod hadn't and wasn't. His mind was still on the voices he had. The bowling changed ends. Macleod walked down to watch the first end bowl being delivered. He was now looking back at where he had been sitting previously. Behind him, previously,

21

had been a large window. As the jack came down along the green, he watched someone moving into position and Billy threw bowls down, along with others. Macleod wasn't really looking.

Billy didn't want any advice on what to bowl, how to bowl, which Macleod quite enjoyed because he didn't have a clue how to bowl, anyway. He stared at the window behind Billy. The day outside was damp and there wasn't a lot of sunshine. Suddenly appearing at the window, Macleod could make out a figure. It was in grey. Totally in grey.

'Mary Smith. Mary Smith. Talk to me about Mary Smith.'

Macleod felt a crack of a whip across him. He felt a punch driving in. He looked down the rink to the window beyond it. There was a grey figure. It was in a monk's habit.

Macleod stood up, pitching himself forward.

'No, no, no,' said Billy. 'You don't come this way down the rink. You don't bloody well come this way. You're meant to stay down there. Normally, you'd be giving me instructions. Seoras, bloody hell. Where are you going?'

'Mary Smith,' said the voice again. 'Take him. Beat it out of him. Beat it out of him.'

The figure was walking across the grass outside the window. He turned and Macleod saw the mask.

'Are you okay, Seoras? Seoras, are you—'

Macleod heard nothing. He was making for the far exit just along from the window. It was an emergency exit with a metal bar across it. If he could hit it with two hands, he'd be out there. He could catch the guy. The killer was here!

They'd chased him, chased him so far, and yet here he was. Macleod would shake the answers from him. Why had he done it to him? Who was he? What was the point?

Macleod took another glance at the window. The figure was there. He was looking at him. Then was it turning? It was going to flee. He wouldn't get away. He wouldn't. Macleod would stop him.

'Halt,' shouted Macleod. 'Police, halt.'

'What the hell? Seoras.' Billy stepped forward, trying to grab Macleod. Almost instinctively, Macleod's hand went out, pushing Billy in the chest. The man stumbled backward and landed with his backside in the middle of his bowls.

'Seoras, calm down. Seoras. Seoras!'

Macleod heard nothing. He didn't need to. Instead, he needed to get out and grab the masked man. He hit the emergency exit with both hands, pushing the doors open. He almost tripped as the step dropped onto the grass outside. Macleod turned to look for him. The man was gone. There was nothing there.

'Seoras! Seoras, calm down. Easy. Breathe easy, Seoras. You're not there. It's okay.'

Margaret was talking to Macleod again. He became aware that she was holding his hand.

'I was just chasing him. He was here. He was here, the man that held me, the man that killed them, the man who tortured me. Did you see him? At the window?' said Macleod.

'There was nobody at the window. Sorry, Seoras. There's nobody out here now, either.'

'He was wearing a grey coat. Actually, a grey habit. Mask, grey mask on.'

'I think we would have seen him. Come on, Seoras. Back inside. You just knocked Billy into the middle of his bowls.'

'Stuff Billy's bowls,' said Macleod. 'He was here. The man was here.'

Macleod looked around him. On the ground was a pamphlet of some sort. A flyer. That's what it was. He bent down and picked it up. He looked at a picture of a boat. It was on fire with the words *vengeance is mine!* above it.

'What's that, Seoras? Oh, that's rubbish. Do you want me to bin that for you?'

'No,' said Macleod. He folded it up and put it in his pocket. He turned round and looked all along the outside of the sports building. There was no one there, but the man had been there. *They wouldn't have seen him, would they? Could they have seen him? What was he doing? It doesn't make sense. Bastard,* thought Macleod. He couldn't trust his own senses. Macleod turned and slowly made his way back inside.

'You shoved me to the ground,' said Billy.

'You get out of the way quicker, then,' said Macleod.

'Do you want a seat, Seoras? We'll get your coffee.'

'Not from this place, you won't.'

'Sounds like somebody's got their faculties back,' said Margaret. 'Good.'

Macleod grimaced. What was real and what wasn't? This was a proper hell.

Chapter 04

The Falls of Shin were cordoned off with several police cars guarding the entrance. Hope noticed that there was another area cordoned off further down the side road. She told Susan to drive up to the main visitor area as Ross had said the bodies were close to it. On arrival, she stepped out of the car and scanned the area. A man in uniform came, walking steadily over towards her.

'Chief Inspector?' he said, questioningly.

'That is a question,' said Hope. 'Detective Inspector Hope McGrath. Normally would be Detective Chief Inspector Seoras Macleod, but—'

'I heard,' said the man. 'Sergeant McKay. I rarely work down in the Inverness station. I'm further up, but we know most of you. Of course, I've seen you on the television and that.'

'You got a first name, Sergeant?' asked Hope.

'Peter.'

'Hi, Peter, I'm Hope. This is DC Susan Cunningham, or Susan to us. We've got Ross at the back. That's DC Alan Ross, but everyone calls him Ross, and the other person getting out is—'

'That's Clarissa Urquhart,' said the man. 'Macleod's Rottweiler.'

'Yes, it is,' said Hope. 'However, we rarely call her that.'

'No, but it's with justification,' said the man.

'Oh,' said Hope. 'Previous run-ins?'

'Worked a case or two with her when she was doing the art squad up around these parts. We have several rather wealthy individuals with land who collect certain items, and some of them weren't collecting them in a very fair way. Very robust lady,' he said. 'Anyway, pleasure to have you here, albeit in rather grim circumstances. If you come with me, I'll show you what we've got so far.'

Sergeant McKay took Hope and Susan Cunningham over to a path that led down towards the Falls of Shin. The day was bright, although there were a few clouds about, so every now and again, the brightness would suddenly go dim as the sun was blocked out. There'd been rain. That fresh smell was in the air, but it was also slightly muggy.

'We've got two cars,' said the Sergeant. 'One in the visitor's car park, one down the road half a mile away. I'm trying to run them through the system, see who they belong to. The one in the visitor's car park is a hire car. However, it's a stolen hire car, taken out of Inverness approximately two weeks ago. Hasn't been seen until now.'

The man pointed to the rope system hanging on a tree that was now leaving a body swinging over the river.

'Your forensic lead, Miss Nakamura, is on scene. They're just working out the best way to bring him back over, pick up any evidence from him.'

'Yes, they haven't left him in an easy place to get at, have they?' said Hope. Rather than offer any theories of her own, she remained silent, leaving issues like that for Jona.

26

'Second body is about a quarter of a mile away, and as you can see with this one, they're both left naked. There are no clothes. The car has got nothing in it. Neither car has. I haven't been able to find any ID. It's all most strange.'

'A guy swinging by a rope naked across the Falls of Shin and some other woman lying naked somewhere in the grass. I'd say it was strange. Well, thanks for that.' Hope looked at Susan. 'Why don't you take a walk down to the other car? See what you can find down there.' Clarissa came marching along the path past Susan, going the other way.

'That him?' asked Clarissa, and then realised the obvious redundancy in the question.

'Yes, that's him,' said Sergeant McKay. 'Good to see you again, Sergeant.'

'It's Petey,' said Clarissa, and the man went suddenly red. 'Petey's not very good on his art, but Petey knows how to drink!'

'There was a large degree of unfairness in that competition,' said Peter.

'No, there wasn't,' said Clarissa. 'You just don't take on a Scottish woman like me.'

'Anyway,' said the man, 'I was just showing your inspector the scene. We haven't been able to pull him back in yet.'

He turned and saw a team of forensic officers now reaching out with some large hook on a pole.

'Looks like they're bringing him back in. Do you want to see Miss Nakamura?'

'Lead on, Petey,' said Clarissa. Hope gave her a sharp look.

'I'll see how close we can get,' said the uniformed officer. He disappeared for a couple of minutes before Jona made her way towards them. She pulled back her hood and gave a rather wry smile.

'Lovely day for it,' she said. 'I had a quick examination of our female friend. I'll be able to get a hold of this guy in a minute.'

'What did you find out?' asked Hope.

'Well, Sergeant's probably told you, there's no ID. Both of them left utterly naked. No clothes, no nothing. From a quick look at the woman, she's probably only about twenty-five, twenty-six. She has got rather flashy fingernails, lipstick and mascara on, made up well, made up to attract.'

'Okay,' said Hope. 'But that doesn't really say a lot. They could have been up here to, what, rendezvous, meet for a—'

'There's something else about her. She has markings around her wrists and ankles that show bondage. She has been strapped around there and fairly recently. Looking at them, I'd say it's a common occurrence because of the hardness around the skin.'

'So, you think she was tied up?' asked Susan.

'That's not what she's saying,' said Hope. 'Is it?'

'No,' said Jona. 'There are also some marks that I would say are from whips or some sort of striking implement, maybe a cane, something like that.'

'A cane?' queried Susan. 'You think somebody thrashed her?'

'No,' said Jona. 'Where these marks are, between the legs, across the chest, across the backside, she looks like a working girl to me. Someone that works with men who like to tie their ladies up a bit. BDSM, bondage, that sort of thing. They're not strong enough to be caused in a less than playful fashion. There's certainly a lot of control with the marks that are there, and a lot of them have been there over time. The skin's hardened. Yes, I would say she was a working girl.'

'So he's out here with a hooker,' said Hope. 'He's brought a

28

prostitute out to here. I mean, the Falls of Shin are nice and that, but I wouldn't have seen them bringing prostitutes out. If you're going to go to a prostitute, surely you go to their room or a hotel room, you don't, what, do it in a car? How did they end up out there? This couldn't have been some sort of sex act, could it?'

'No,' said Jona. 'I mean—' Then she stopped.

'No,' said Susan. 'The logistics of trying to do anything sexual where he is at the moment—'

'Precisely,' said Jona. Sergeant McKay looked rather embarrassed by everything.

'You've got to live a little, Sergeant. See all things in this line of work. It's not the art world,' teased Clarissa.

Sergeant McKay gave a nod, then asked to be excused, saying he'd be talking to the station from his car in the car park if he was required. Hope gave a wry smile as he walked off. Couldn't have been easy for a man surrounded by four women.

'If you put some outfits on, we'll take a look at our man now that they've brought him back from across the river. Otherwise, you can wait here and hear from me.'

'I'll let you go back,' said Hope, 'come and see you in about five minutes when you've had a quick look. I want to get on to organising a stop and search, see what's going on, if anybody's seen anything.'

'We're quite remote here,' said Clarissa.

'We are, so maybe we want to take a bit of a wider scan. The woman's body's and out beyond. Is there anything more? Susan, talk to McKay, get a couple of uniforms, and search down the tracks that lead out from here, but not onto the main road. The tracks that lead further away. Quick search just to see if anything else is lying around.'

29

'Will do,' she said.

'Clarissa,' said Hope. 'Talk to uniform, see where it would be useful to do stop-and-ask checks. See the likelihood of traffic around here, anybody likely to be driving home, maybe returning from Inverness as they are working down there. You know the deal.'

Clarissa nodded. 'You want the naked man all to yourself?'

'Yes, we missed you,' said Hope.

Clarissa stomped off. Hope stood looking at where the man had been hanging before. Why hang him out there? What is he? Why do this? Was this a continuation of the other minister and corporate killings? If it was, it was bizarre. With those, everything was always done in public, everything was a show, everything was trying to say something. Now here, it's remote, it's away. It didn't look like it was the same killer. Jona returned five minutes later, shaking her head.

'Very little to say. He's probably an office worker, as he's got soft hands. There are no marks on him except for his buttocks and the sides of his legs. Looks like he's been scraped along, but that's to be expected. They had to drag him here somehow. Looks like he's died because his neck's been broken. Possibly on the drop-off there. If you look across, where could that rope have dropped from? Possibly that outcrop over there. You can get to it easily from the path.'

'Would you need a team of people to put him there?'

'You need to secure the rope. If you had that done that in advance, no. If you're able to restrain him, no. Could you have put the noose around and lifted him, dragged him up to that rock? It would be easier done with several people, but a strong person, they could do it on their own.'

'Any idea about time of death? Was it similar for both of

30

them? Was it far apart?'

'It's hard to be that precise,' said Jona, 'but there's nothing to say they wouldn't have been around the same time.'

'Excellent,' said Hope. 'Well, I'll let you do your work. See if you can find out anything else about him for me. I take it you're going through the cars as well.'

'We are doing, to see who's been in what.'

'The woman who died?' asked Hope.

'Strangled, just strangled. The guy's got reasonable hands, not small, not uncommonly large either, from what I could tell. I'll get a closer examination. But she had the life throttled clean out of her. I think she had something in her mouth though or she'd have screamed.'

Hope walked back up the track to the main car park at the Falls of Shin. The visitor centre was dark, remaining locked, except for one door that was open. Inside, she saw Sergeant McKay. He had commandeered a small table. It's a good idea Because Hope felt the rain could come at any time. As she stood there, she saw Susan Cunningham coming back up, and getting a hold of Ross. The two approached her.

'We found something in the car down below,' said Susan. 'It belongs to an Eamon Banner.'

'And Eamon Banner is?'

'Well, I looked up him on the systems. He's classified as a civil servant, but he's flagged.'

'What do you mean, flagged?' asked Hope.

'Intelligence. He's a low-level intelligence officer.'

'Have you told them?'

'Just reported it. Guess we might see some of them about.'

'Yes,' said Hope. 'Gut feeling,' she said to the pair of them. 'I thought at first this might be our killer, the one that put Seoras

31

in the funny farm. But it all feels different. It all feels wrong. This could be another matter. Go through the investigation, go through the procedures, do the work, keep an open mind.'

Hope looked at Susan Cunningham. 'Yes,' said Hope. 'Don't jump to conclusions.'

Chapter 05

He was hanging, his wrists secured to a post. His bare torso was hovering over a cold stone floor and his arms were spread like wings of an angel. Yet, he certainly wasn't in heaven.

Around him he could see was fire; orange and red, intermingled with the occasional yellow. And the heat. The heat was so strong. Sweat dripped off his brow, ran down his nose, dripped from his chin onto his chest. His chest was on fire. He saw thick cut lines where a whip had bedded in, only to be drawn away and leave a red in the middle of two shores. His feet were together and gripped tight by some sort of manacle.

Left and right through the flames, he could see masks. Masks slid off faces, but there were no features on the faces behind them. Time and time again he peered, desperate to glimpse who was behind, but nothing. In the crack of another whip, someone stepped forward with a spear dressed in a grey habit and that damned mask again. He pulled back the spear, drove it towards Macleod, and then a pair of hands caught it.

He looked up and saw the red hair. *Should be in a ponytail*, he thought. *She doesn't wear it in a ponytail when she's out, but this is work. It should be in a ponytail.*

He saw Hope grab the spear, pull it from the man's hands, and throw it away. She then hit him, knocking them back into the flames. Instead of burning, the man seemed to vanish to be replaced by another one, this time from his right-hand side. He watched this repeatedly. A new figure would approach, spear in hand, aiming for him, and every time the woman before him would fight them off.

Macleod woke with a start. He looked around the room. He was lying in his bed in the care home. A pitcher of water was on the left-hand side, a bland picture of flowers was on the wall. His pyjama top was lying over the chair. Everything was as he left it, everything in its place when he'd gone to sleep.

He'd clearly been upset at the bowling. Clearly, something had got a hold of his mind. These flashbacks were killing him. He wasn't in control. He wasn't in charge of them.

He'd be going to see a shrink, or a psychologist, as they called it. They were always shrinks, however, in the office. There'd been shrinks back in the day when he first joined, although there hadn't been as many back then. People back then seemed to have dealt with their problems. No, that wasn't correct, was it? People back then had compartmentalised them, packaged them up and stuck them to some part of the brain that didn't want to look at them.

He'd known that, for he'd seen it too often. He'd seen past terrors come back to haunt people's actions. Macleod needed to get rid of this. How could you think straight if all you could think about was the terror that was happening around you? Macleod sat up on the bed, swung his legs round and stood up.

He walked over to the window, pulled back the curtains, and saw several of his fellow patients sitting outside. It must have brightened, and he gave a smile as he watched them before closing the curtain again, suddenly aware that his torso was bare.

He looked down at his body, half expecting to see gorges of red across him, but there weren't. There were scars. Some of them were deep. There were welts that had formed, but there was no standing blood. The skin had healed up over that.

Macleod walked over to the pitcher of water, poured himself a glass and drank. He was tired. He felt like the legs were going to go from underneath him. Placing the glass back down beside the pitcher, he turned and walked back to his bed and sat down on the edge for a moment. He tried to think about the nightmare he just had.

Why? he thought, *why in the middle of people attacking me do I only manage the focus on the fact that her hair isn't in a ponytail? She suits it with her hair down, she always did. She was more like working Hope when the ponytail was intact. That was the Hope he knew. The Hope he relied on.*

McGrath and he had started awkwardly, but they had formed a unique friendship. Once they got past the differences.

Macleod looked over at his bedside. There was a photograph of a smiling woman, but it wasn't Hope. Jane was staring back at him. He sometimes thought of them as his two women, his professional partner and his partner. He absently once thought of her as his home partner. She had a greater status than that. Jane and he were well suited. They were a genuine couple.

She knew his weaknesses, could find them, dig them out, support him in them, back him up. She brought out the joy in him he didn't know he had inside, but she also knew that when he went to work, she lost him. Jane lost him to this

35

young redhead, not in any physical way, not in any way that threatened what they had between them, but he was lost to the case and the team. Lost to the need to discover what was going on, and in that, Hope was the supporter. Hope was the one that stood beside him.

Macleod gave a little laugh. 'But her hair should be tied up,' he said aloud. 'Always tied up, because when her hair's down, that's when she's John's.'

He was happy for Hope. When he first knew her, he could tell she was looking for someone, something. She was unsettled. Some people were like that. He'd come across enough people in his lifetime to know there were those who desperately needed someone to love them. There were those who found others and made it work. There were those who didn't need anyone and were in it for other reasons, and there were those who just weren't bothered.

Hope had needed someone. She always lacked that bit of surety, that complete confidence in herself. He knew he wasn't always good at building that. Macleod worked differently. He came at things from a different angle, an angle that sometimes made her think he was some sort of superstar.

Hope was a plotter. She grafted, dug out the clues. Hope really worked at getting there. In truth, she was more like Clarissa, just less brutal with it. Hope had a subtlety about her, a subtlety that a six-foot redhead didn't need. Macleod laughed once again, swung his legs back underneath the covers and decided he needed to get back to sleep. It took a while, but slowly he drifted off.

Jane was there. Jane had appeared this time, and Macleod was out on the riverbank with her. They were walking along. He was laughing, something they said he didn't do at work.

Macleod knew how to laugh. More than that, Jane knew how to make him laugh. She could poke out the problems to show him where he was being daft. Show him where he was flawed, but without being accusatory or too sympathetic. She was a challenge and an encouragement all at once.

They walked along the riverbank, staring at the ducks as they went past. Then he turned a corner, and she wasn't with him. Before him was a street he knew well. There was a police station on the left-hand side. One he'd been to not that long ago.

This was Stornoway. This was the police station that he'd first been posted to. *Yes*, he thought, this is that station; not the modern one. The original building. The fixture he stepped into as a constable.

He walked up the steps, opened the door and saw McNeil going the other way. The man was younger, not the old man he'd seen in the care home. Macleod gave a quick heels-together as McNeil walked past, and then he turned towards where the desk sergeant was. The man was on the phone.

'Everything okay?' asked Macleod.

'No,' said the desk sergeant. 'Who is Mary Smith? Tell me, who is Mary Smith?'

'Mairi?'

'No, Mary Smith. Who is Mary Smith?'

McNeil was beside him.

'We don't need to know about Mary Smith.'

'Mary is okay.'

'Mary is gone,' he said. 'Mary's going away. Think about Mairi, not Mary,' said McNeil.

Macleod turned and walked further into the station, opening a door that was old and wooden. He stepped through into what should have been a corridor, but it was a ring of fire.

Macleod looked down at the shirt he'd been wearing. His police uniform was gone. He was in his underpants, his arms tied behind him. Beside him was a mass of hair. He looked at the hair. It was a red ponytail.

Beyond the ring of fire there were many grey figures in habits, all with masks on, the same mask taunting now.

'Macleod, sinner,' they yelled. 'Pay for your sins. Pay for your sins, Macleod. What would God think of you? Don't you know? Weren't you taught when you grew up?'

Macleod was taught. He knew that, but this, this was just—

He watched as someone came through the fire. They pushed Hope aside. She stumbled and fell, and then the man turned with a spear, driving it straight into Macleod's heart.

Seoras Macleod awoke with a start, sitting upright in bed, sweat pouring down his face. Then he saw him.

A masked figure in front of him, dressed in grey, lifted his hand. The finger pointed at Macleod. It was a man. It had that unmistakable bulk, but there were none of the facial features available, all hidden behind the mask.

'You,' the figure said. 'You, Macleod, you haven't paid for your guilt. Mary Smith. Mary Smith!'

'I don't know a Mary Smith. Please, I didn't know a Mary Smith. I wasn't there with a Mary Smith.'

'You haven't paid for your guilt, Macleod, and if you haven't paid, then the innocent will pay. You stopped me with fire last time, and with fire, I'll repay what's due. I'll repay Macleod, and remember, it's your guilt that brought this all on. Guilty. Guilty. Guilty.'

The man chanted the word, standing almost motionless, his finger pointing straight at Macleod.

It must be a dream. It must be a nightmare, thought Macleod. He reached forward, but the man was beyond him.

'Guilty. Guilty. Guilty.'

'Stop it,' said Macleod. 'Stop saying it. Stop saying the word. Don't.'

'I will burn with fire. Repay what's due, Macleod. I will do this and you will pay for your price of your failure.'

'Get out!' shouted Macleod. 'Staff! Someone, get him out, get him out of this room. I don't want him in this room. Tell him to go. Get him out, get him out!'

Sweat was pouring off Macleod's body now, but inside he was cold, numb at this finger pointed at him. The figure just kept pointing. Macleod swung his legs around off the bed, tried to propel himself up onto his feet, but by the time he stood upright and turn, the figure was gone.

'He's getting away. Someone, someone he's getting away!'

Macleod tried to rush forward. His foot caught a slipper lying in his path, and he tumbled to the ground.

'Help!' he cried. 'Help, he's getting away. The man's getting away!'

A young woman raced in, dressed in green scrubs, jumped over Macleod, and knelt down beside him.

'Seoras, are you okay? Did you take a fall?'

'He's getting away, I tell you. You need to go after him. Stop him. Stop him!'

'Who?' asked the woman.

'No, don't. Don't go after him,' said Macleod. 'It'll be bad for you. Phone, phone Hope. Tell her to get the uniform down here. 9-9-9, whatever, just phone them.'

The woman continued to kneel beside him. 'You are shivering,' she said. 'You're cold and numb. Let's get you up to bed.'

'No!' shouted Macleod. 'He was here. He was here!'

'There was no one here,' said the woman. 'I've just come in. There was no one here. I didn't see anybody leave.'

'No,' said Macleod on the floor. 'No, he was here. It was real. He told me, he said Mary Smith. I told him Mairi, I only know Mairi. It's—'

A second figure arrived in the room and together the staff half lifted Macleod back to the bed. They swung his legs in and covered up his body with sheets.

'I'll get the doctor to come and look at you. It will take a while because they've got to come from the surgery, but I think it warrants a look.'

Macleod nodded his head, but he wasn't listening to the helper beside him. Instead, his mind and his eyes were focused on the end of the bed. *What had been there? It was someone real.* Macleod could have sworn it was.

After the helper had finished speaking, she turned and left the room and Macleod glanced over at the small table beside his bed. On top of it was a sheet of paper, the one he picked up. It had the words *Vengeance is mine* on it. *Had he been imagining this? Was he going daft? Twice today. Twice,* he thought.

I can't lose my mind, he said to himself. *I can't. My mind is me. I'll be nothing without it.*

Chapter 06

'So when you were younger, did you come to these sorts of places? I mean—'

'These sorts of places,' said Ross, looking carefully towards Cunningham. 'I'm not really into women.'

'I know that,' said Susan, 'but they must have catered for male tastes as well.'

'Not so much,' said Ross, 'and besides, this is not the sort of place I would have come.'

'Oh well, I had a few boyfriends who seemed to like to take me to places like this.'

'Places like this? Seriously?' said Ross, shocked.

'Yes. Well, maybe not places like this, more so the conventional strip joints and that. Seemed to enjoy me sitting there with them while they were ogling away.'

'And you were okay with that?'

'No, not really. I mean, there's plenty to look at here, isn't there?' Susan Cunningham turned round, opened her jacket up, and stood in a rather seductive pose towards Ross.

'Probably asking the wrong person,' said Ross. 'Anyway, enough of that, let's just get on, shall we?'

'I was just having a bit of fun, just trying to get to know you,'

41

said Susan. 'Rarely do you and I get out together on our own. I mean, I'm surprised I'm not out here with Clarissa.'

'Hope said she wanted to find any missing girls. It requires a degree of subtly talking to these sorts of people. Clarissa doesn't like them. I think she'd be quite hostile towards them.'

'What, and you like them?'

'Of course not,' said Ross, 'I just have a—well, let's say I have more decorum about how I go about things.'

'And what am I here for?'

'I could be nasty and say eye candy,' said Ross. 'Maybe just leg work.'

'What do you mean by that?' Said Susan.

'Susan, you've not been on the team that long. Sometimes you need to see how we go about this sort of thing. You've got to trawl, you've got to speak to the people you don't want to speak to, see what you can find out.'

'You said eye candy first.'

'Well, look at it this way. If I come in with Clarissa, are these people going to speak to us? Probably only if Clarissa throttles them. So, you're going to have to put the boot in somehow, give them an incentive that way. Put somebody good-looking on with me, and they might give you a few words at least. Not that it will get you everywhere, but Hope knows this. Hope knows how to play people. She learned that from Macleod. Macleod's used her before.'

'That's sexist,' said Susan.

'No, it's understanding who's in front of you. These guys, they look at women all the time, they treat them as sex objects. In fact, they make money out of them. We're going to people that run, frankly, rather dodgy brothels. If you don't think they're looking at you as something they can make a profit out of, and sexually, you're not much of a detective. Before you ask, if it was a brothel full of male prostitutes, yes, she would use me in the same way.'

'Yes, but you don't have the looks.'

Ross stared at Cunningham and saw a cheeky grin. She'd got him. She'd totally got him.

'Not to worry,' he said. 'Come on, in here.'

Ross opened the door into a back alley. Walking down it, Cunningham could see a large bouncer at the end. The man must have been about six feet four, as wide as any brick house she'd ever seen, but Ross walked straight up to him.

'DC Alan Ross, this is DC Susan Cunningham. We're investigating some recent murders, and we're concerned about the safety of the girls within your employ.'

'There're no women employed here,' said the man.

'No, maybe there isn't, but the women that live here could be in trouble, so I'd like to speak to your boss.'

'The boss doesn't like to speak to people. He's busy.'

'I can appreciate that,' said Ross. 'It's a very hidden establishment, this one, isn't it?'

The big man stared at him, snarling.

'And the thing is that you won't lay a finger on us, not two constables, not standing in the doorway like this. You'll calmly tell us we can't come in, tell us to get a warrant, which is fine. All perfectly within your rights, but you won't lay a finger on us unless we try to go through that door. Of course, I won't barge in through the door when told I can't come in, but there's another thing you should concern yourself with.'

'And what would that be?' the man growled at Ross.

'If your boss chooses not to see me right now, I will march out to the front of here, I will get some placards, I will march round and round, shouting, "Stop the brothels." I will get lots more people here to join me, and I will make sure that everybody knows what this place is. Make sure that there's a good leafleted campaign about all the people who come here, and how they give your boss their money.'

'He's right,' said Susan. 'I'll be there with him, women's rights and all that.'

The large man spat in the ground, 'Just get out of here before you know what's good for you.'

'You lay a finger on me,' said Ross, 'and she'll take you down. You won't even see it coming.'

'She doesn't scare me. Look at her, there's nothing to her.'

'Try, seriously, makes our job a lot easier. We can take you down to the station and have a good chat with you. Your boss won't be happy. Tell him I'm here. Tell him I'm here or I'm going to make a nuisance of myself. I'm not coming for him. I need to know that all your women are safe.'

The man turned away reluctantly, opened the door, but not before he turned around and gave a weird leer over his shoulder.

'She'll take you down,' said Susan, quietly. 'You really believe that I could take him down?'

'No,' said Ross, 'I really wasn't looking for a fight because I think the two of us would end up battered and bruised. To be quite honest, I've had enough of that lately, but he's off for his boss. If Hope had been here, I would have used that threat properly.'

'You think the boss has got a better punch than me?'

'I know she has.'

'But what about Clarissa? Would you have said it if she was here?'

44

'No,' said Ross. 'She'd have killed him.'

Cunningham stared in shock. The bouncer returned and opened the door giving a gruff, 'This way.' Ross smiled at Cunningham and stepped inside.

They went through to a winding staircase of a house. In many rooms, they could hear elicit sexual activity. Ross tried to make a note of as much as possible to pass it on when he got back to the station to the relevant units, but they probably knew about most of it already. The difficulty was proving things, catching the big ringleaders. For the minute, what he needed to do was find out were there any girls missing.

'This had better be good,' said a man behind a desk as Ross was introduced to a room at the top of the building.

'It's not good. That's why I'm here,' said Ross. 'DC Alan Ross, DC Susan Cunningham. We're investigating some murders that happened recently at the Falls of Shin.'

'Shin? That's miles up north. What are you coming looking at me for the Falls of Shin for? I don't have any of my girls at the Falls of Shin. There are no punters up there. It's a ridiculous idea.'

'That would indeed be a ridiculous idea. However, one of the dead people at the Falls of Shin, we believe to be a prostitute, a female prostitute.'

'Well, I haven't got any of my girls missing. They're all here, all accounted for, so you can get back out, DC Ross.'

'I'd like to talk to them,' said Ross. 'I'd like to talk to them to see if any have been approached by someone. This looks like a contract job. Looks like someone was hired to go up north to Shin, and they paid with it for their life. I want to know who's attacking your girls.'

'No. You don't get to talk to them. Not alone.'

45

'Look,' said Ross. 'I could go away, come back and bust this place apart. But by the time I do that, you'll have moved everything incriminating. You'll have done a runner, and we'll have got absolutely no access to any of your girls. We'll have found nothing out and you would have the biggest headache in your business you've had in a long time. Doesn't work for either of us. I talk to them now; find out what I need to know. I may even stop someone from taking them away from you and what's the worst you lose, five, ten minutes of their time?'

'Some of them are busy at the moment.'

The man behind the desk had a large moustache and Ross couldn't help thinking that he was involved in the '70s cheap porn film industry. He had such a strange look, especially with the medallion that hung around his neck. But for all the comical look, he would be a businessman. These people invariably were.

'I will not speak to anyone who's with someone. We will wait until they come out,' said Ross, 'but I want to speak to them all.'

'Maybe your partner could look around,' said the man. 'See if she prefers this sort of work.'

'You were right,' said Susan.

'What do you mean?' asked the man.

'He said you'd be looking at me. He said you'd be thinking about me in here. Ross knows his men.'

Ross couldn't look at Cunningham, knowing that was a jibe. 'Do we get to interview anyone?' asked Ross, 'or do I have to get my warrant?'

'One by one, take your time. Interrupt no one. The big man will stay with you. Make sure they don't talk about me.'

'That's fine,' said Ross, 'but I'm warning him. If he interrupts

46

the requirements of our investigation and stops them from answering about that, I'll let Cunningham take him apart.'

The big man was at the door and looked over at Susan. Susan looked up at him and gave a smile.

'No need for that, officer. He's just protecting my interests.'

It took the best part of two hours to get through all the girls. Ross had made notes of names. Most of them, he believed, would be false, but in case he had to come back again, at least he'd know who he was talking to. The last girl came in and Ross guessed she must have been, at most, nineteen or twenty. She looked shy and was dressed in just a T-shirt and tracksuit bottoms.

'You a local fitness instructor?' asked Ross.

'Day off,' said the girl.

'What's your name?' asked Susan.

'Emma. Emma Cobain.'

'Well, Emma,' said Susan, 'have you noticed anything strange recently? Anything strange from clients? We think one of your kind's been killed up near the Falls of Shin. Hired out. Just wanting to know if you'd had any unusual requests to do a job elsewhere.'

'I have done,' she said. 'I have done.' The big man looked over at her, grunting.

'Well, Donny said I could do it. Donny said he wanted twenty-five percent of the take, but he said I could do it.' The girl stared at the big man, who looked like he was about to intervene physically.

'What's going on here?' asked Ross.

'Mark here,' said Emma, 'is trying to stop me talking about this because he thinks it's business, Donny's business. Donny knew next to nothing about it.'

47

'Do you want to explain?'

Again, there was a grunt from the big man. Ross turned round to him.

'Look, if you've got a problem with this, get Donny down here. Okay? If you don't, either shut up or get out.'

The man walked over towards Ross, cracked his knuckles, got close to Ross's face. 'I'm warning you, officer.'

There was a sudden crack of knuckles behind him. He turned and saw Susan Cunningham standing there poised, ready to strike the man. 'That would be unwise,' she said. 'Very unwise.'

'No need for this. Either get Donny or let us get on with this,' said Ross.

'Mark, don't worry,' said Emma, 'it's got nothing to do with the business. There's nothing that's going to incriminate Donny. I just need to tell them this because I was spooked.'

'Does Donny know you were spooked?' asked Ross.

'I just told him it was a dead end. You don't talk to your boss about other jobs you were doing, even if he has sanctioned them.'

'Go on,' said Ross.

'Well,' said Emma, 'I was asked to do a job by a man in a bar. I think he'd followed me from here. He said it was significant money, and it was. He gave me a bit of a down payment, and he said that he needed me to come up north for a bit and entertain a man. Basically, it would be out in the open. A job in a car near some waterfall. Apparently he liked the open air and all that stuff. I said okay, arranged it and took the money, okayed it with Donny. But when I got to the car to be picked up, the man who was hiring me said that his client liked it rough.'

'Rough?' asked Susan, 'and you're okay with that?'

'There's rough and there's rough,' said the woman. 'I asked him what he meant. You know, some guys just like it to be very physical. There's a big difference between that and—well, and abuse.'

Ross was wondering just where the line of abuse fell, considering the job the woman was in, but he didn't want to interrupt the flow.

'The thing is, he started talking about being tied up and being hit with chains and whips. Only not in that sort of comical way. He was talking—'

'Scared you, did it?' asked Susan. 'It would scare me.'

'I got out of there as fast as I could. You just don't risk something like that. Wants to drive me up North, wants to do all this? No. Threw his money at him and ran.'

'Could you describe him?' asked Ross.

'Not really. He was wearing a large coat at the time. Bit of a hat. Didn't see his hair, saw little of his face. It was in the dark when he spoke to me, but he was well set. He was commanding, and he had this weird Scottish accent I couldn't actually place.'

'Where are you from?' asked Ross.

'England,' said Emma. 'I get the Glasgow twang and that, and you hear the accents. Even up here in Inverness, you can—-I'd recognise that accent, but this one was from somewhere else. And he said a word. He said a word that baffled me.'

'What do you mean?' Asked Ross.

'When you do this job, some guys don't take a liking to this, that, or whatever. You get many words thrown at you. The usual ones, tart and much worse, but this guy said something else.'

'What'd he say?' asked Ross.

49

'Salachair!'

'What does that mean?' asked Ross.

'Don't know,' said Emma, 'I don't know, but he said it three times, and each time he did, I ran faster.'

Chapter 07

Hope had sent Cunningham and Ross out to track down any information about the deceased woman. This left her going through some reports back at the office. Clarissa was out in the other office chasing up the co-opted uniformed officers and Patterson. They were waiting on any more findings from Jona Nakamura, and inquiries into details about Eamon Banner. Hope knew he was a low-level operative in the intelligence organisations, but she didn't know exactly who.

Deep in the paperwork, her phone rang on the desk, and she picked it up, hearing a woman's voice on the other end.

'Hello. I'd like to speak to DCI Macleod.'

'Macleod isn't here now. I'm afraid Seoras is indisposed. You're speaking to DI Hope McGrath. Can I assist you?'

'You can indeed. My name is unimportant, but I have some information for you. Macleod would usually talk to me when he needed some help. I'd like to meet up with you on the shores of Loch Ness, somewhere around the Dores area.'

'What?' blurted Hope. 'The Dores area? Why would you want to meet up with me in the Dores area? Who is this?'

'It's someone with information. Information that could

help you. Also, we need to work together. All you need to remember is Kirsten Stewart would approve of this meeting.'

Hope suddenly stopped, half looking at the papers on her desk and focused in on the call fully.

'Excuse me? You know Kirsten Stewart?'

'Yes,' said the woman. 'I'll meet you at Dores on the shores of Loch Ness. Let's say an hour.'

'Let's not—' The phone line had gone dead on the other end.

Hope looked rather bemusedly at the phone before putting the receiver back down. She stood up, turned, looked out of the window, and pondered on the call. She then took a walk to her office door, opened it, and shouted for Clarissa to join her. When Clarissa came in, Hope relayed the phone call to her word for word.

'Let's go then.'

'Let's go then?' queried Hope. 'What do you mean?'

'Let's go then. Said she knew Kirsten Stewart. She was the one here before me. Knows Kirsten; has information. Let's go.'

'You don't find it strange they didn't give their name?'

'You said Kirsten went off to the secret services. No, I don't find it strange. Let's go, but I'll keep a distance between you and me, make it look like you've come alone.'

'Okay,' said Hope. 'Well, first sign of trouble, we'll walk out of this one. No calvary charges from yourself.'

'I think my charging days are done,' said Clarissa. 'Take my car?'

'We're going in quietly,' said Hope, 'so, no. We'll take mine.'

Hope dropped Clarissa a short distance away before parking the car up and walking onto the rocky beach at Dores. Loch Ness was looking particularly fine with a break in the clouds casting light on the far side of the loch. However, the trees on the near side caused a shadow over the beach. She wasn't alone because there were the other occasional walkers, but Hope couldn't see anyone hanging around.

The woman had said an hour; it had been fifty-nine minutes. Surely somebody would be here by now. Hope waited longer, and then, precisely a minute later, a woman in a black suit marched onto the beach. She was wearing what would probably be described as a man's shoe, but given the terrain they were on, it was certainly effective. Her black hair was not tied up, swinging around her shoulders, and Hope placed her probably towards the top end of forty. Maybe even slightly older, but she was in good shape and certainly looked like she could move if she had to.

'Detective Inspector,' said the woman. 'Strange meeting you.'

'Maybe it is,' said Hope. I am at a loss. What's your name?'

'My name doesn't matter. What does matter is that I know a lot about Eamon Banner, and Eamon Banner was a low-level intelligence officer.'

'And how did you know him?' asked Hope.

'I'm not at liberty to say, but you should know that Eamon Banner is of great importance, and I'll need to know about this investigation.'

'You need to know?' queried Hope. 'Would you like to give me an address to send a report to?'

'Don't get facetious with me,' said the woman. 'I'll call you. We'll come back here, you can tell me what's what, and then we'll go again.'

'I'll just tell you, even though I don't know who you are? You come and tell me you know a lot about Eamon Banner, but you don't tell me anything about him. You tell me nothing

53

except that I have to come and give you information. Last I understood, your name wasn't DCI Macleod or the Assistant Chief Constable. Therefore, we'll not be talking, and I'd like you to come to the station with me to tell me all you know about Eamon Banner.'

'I'll call you when I need to know some more information,' said the woman. 'Thank you for your assistance, I'll be going.'

She turned, and Hope said, 'Stop. I would like for you to come with me down to the station. I'm telling you to stop now.'

The woman continued to walk. Hope made for her, reaching out to grab her, but the woman's hand shot out, grabbed Hope's, turned her, and drove it up behind her back. There was a crunch of stones as out of the trees ran Clarissa, half hobbling as she came because of previous injuries.

'You didn't come alone then. That's wise,' said the woman.

'Secret Service,' said Clarissa. 'She's secret service, I know her.'

'And you are rather poor at hiding,' said the woman. She let Hope's wrist descend back around, and Hope replaced a grimace on her face with a half-smile. She turned back to face the woman.

'So what was all that all about?' she asked. 'You clearly speak to Macleod at times. I could give Seoras a ring right now, just check out who you are.'

'I wanted to see the sort of person I'm dealing with,' said the woman. 'I don't give away information just like that. Your colleague is correct. I am in the service. Clarissa Urquhart, isn't it?' Hope could see Clarissa's face getting slightly angry.

'And you still haven't said who you are.'

'My name is Anna Hunt. I spoke to Seoras several times

whenever our paths crossed. They're crossing again this time. You need to understand that Eamon Banner was a low-level security person, but he disappeared off with certain vessel movement plans.'

'He what? Can you put that in English?'

'He's taken information to understand where certain boats will be at certain times of the year. He's also noted when various very, very important persons will be on those boats.'

'Very, very important persons,' said Clarissa. 'What's a very, very important person?'

'His majesty, prime minister, the first minister, the—well, you get the drift. Visiting state officials, you know.'

'And you think he's given these away?'

'He's taken them when he hasn't been given access to them. That's the important bit. This is not something he worked with. Eamon worked in other areas. He would've had to have stolen this information. He's stolen it for someone. I believe you have a dead prostitute,' said Anna.

'Mr Banner was someone with a desire for the slightly different. I don't judge people on their preferences, but his was quite strong, and he certainly was the outdoor type when it came to sex. The trouble is that the potential risk from the information going out is low, but if someone were planning something, it could be useful. I'm not worried at this point about what it's going to be used for. But I'm not at a stage of knowing why someone wants it and wants it enough to kill him. Why not just buy him off?

'He won't have gone there to die. He'll have gone there for a good time. Would he be daft enough to get this information for a prostitute? Possibly. The main thing of note,' said Anna, 'is that I need to be kept informed about all that happens. I'll do

55

this by contacting you. We'll meet somewhere like this. Don't bring any notes. We'll talk about what's happened. If I have further information from my side, I'll let you know.'

'Was he based up here?' asked Hope.

'I don't talk about where my people are based, where they've been, but if I have something I can tell you, I will.'

'Doesn't seem very two-way this,' said Hope.

'No, it's not,' said Anna, 'but I work in a very different world.'

'How's Kirsten Stewart?' asked Hope. Anna turned on her heel and walked away. Then she stopped and turned back.

'Macleod's much better at this. He understands things. Bit of discretion. Also, be able to get things out of me, ask in a better way.'

'Are you wanting politeness?' asked Hope.

'No, subtlety. You must have a mind in there,' said Anna. 'Use it. Macleod sent Kirsten to me, not you. Can understand that. You're too methodical. You're too obvious. Although you look like you can handle yourself with a bit of training.'

'I asked how Kirsten Stewart was,' said Hope.

'Yes, you did, and I don't speak about where any of my people are. Good to meet you though,' said Anna.

This time she turned with very deliberate purpose and marched across the beach, feet crunching on the stones. Hope went to go after her, but felt a powerful arm from Clarissa.

'No, no, that's not how it works. If she's here, there's probably several other people here with her. They would take you out before you could get near her. As you're a police officer, they'll probably do it quietly, just lift you somewhere, but you certainly wouldn't get within ten feet of her.'

'She appears to be alone.'

'In that case, that's probably worse,' said Clarissa.

'You've met these people?' asked Hope.

'I have,' said Clarissa. 'The art world's a funny one because of the amount of money involved. Sometimes you meet people from walks of life you wouldn't expect. You cannot get anything out of that one. She's quiet, she's sullen.'

'She might be all that, but we're the police. We're here to help and assist. Doesn't matter what they are. If she wants to work as a team, we'll work as a team. She can't just march in like that on me.'

'It's the only way they're going to march in on you. She must like you, though. She gave you her name.'

'What was all that about testing, then?'

'They're careful with what they say,' said Clarissa, 'but at the end of the day, we know her name. Banner was passing off vessel movement secrets about very, very important people. That's got to be worth something,' said Clarissa. 'Maybe Als can do a job on that on the computer.'

'Good idea,' said Hope. 'I'm going to have a word with Jim. If the Secret Service are going to come and talk to us, we really need to be doing it on a more even footing.'

Clarissa stepped to one side and look back at Hope. 'You are kidding me, aren't you? Seriously, what did you expect? A welcome wagon?'

'She could have popped into the station.'

'No, she couldn't. Come on, boss,' said Clarissa, 'let's get back and get this murder solved.'

Chapter 08

Seoras Macleod felt the water run over his back, and the heat soaking into his shoulders. He rolled them, trying to let out some of the knots and ease the tension that was inside of him. The day had been too much. They said there had been no figure. No person at the end of his bed. He was sure of it. It had seemed so real.

The dreams had been horrible. Terrifying in some ways, but they were dreams. At the end of the day, a dream was a dream. There were those people who tried to read into them, but Macleod believed that his were obvious. He'd been caught in an unpleasant situation and it kept coming back in his dreams. While he didn't enjoy it, he could live with that knowledge. It was something that surely would slip away with time.

The figure at the end of his bed, the figure at the window when bowling, all these things, were they hallucinations? Were they in his mind, active during the day, not just the brain resetting itself at night in a dream?

Macleod turned and let the water hit his chest, rubbing the soap across it. His fingers felt the marks left by the whips. The marks left from beatings. His body was far from recovered, never mind his mind. It would surely only be recovered if one

58

day all those scars left. But they wouldn't leave, would they? They were part of him. Every time he'd climb into bed with Jane, she would see the scars.

He'd always believed that the scar on Hope's face was one of the most beautiful things he'd seen. She'd got it by protecting Jane. A man trying to throw Jane into an acid bath. Something splashed. Hope had caught it on her face and been permanently scarred since then.

He knew many people thought it was a great shame. At 6 feet tall, with long red hair, and in good physical shape, Hope was a good-looking woman. He'd heard the comments, the pity about the face, shame about that, words that angered him. He was lucky, though.

His facial injuries would heal. There'd been bruising, there'd been cuts, but his face would return to normal. Where the whips had hit on the chest and the back, he'd always be marked, but he could always cover those up with a shirt. Nobody would see his damage. His scars would remain underneath, at least as long as he could control what he saw. He could hardly remain disguised if he yelled and screamed at the man at the end of the bed who didn't exist.

There'd been that leaflet, he thought to himself, *that leaflet he'd found on the ground. Vengeance is mine. Fire. They'd never found him,* Macleod thought. *We never got him. Is he still out there? Had he come to torment him?*

What bothered Seoras the most was the fact he had done nothing wrong. Mary Smith. That's all he got was Mary Smith. He didn't know a Mary Smith. Mairi Smith had done well in life. She was fine, as far as he knew. Maybe that was something he'd have to check, but no. She was never called Mary. She was always Mairi.

Macleod watched the steam rise from the shower, disappearing up to the fan. The water ran down in rivulets on the side of the shower. The hair on his legs was streamlined straight down to his feet. He could stay here for a while, for it was good to feel the soft soak of the water. Good to rub the body down with generous quantities of soap. Leave the rest of the world out there. Just take in the gentle massage of the falling water.

Macleod could smell smoke. He looked around him. There'd been clouds of steam rising from the shower, water vapour, but now they'd seemed to grow denser. He began to choke and cough within the cubicle. Something was on fire. But there was only water falling down. There was only Macleod and a couple of bottles of shampoos and soaps.

He spun round, looking at the steam. No. It wasn't steam, was it? It was definitely smoke. It was getting thicker.

He crouched down, taking his head out of the thick smoke at the top into clearer air at the bottom. He looked through the glass of the shower cubicle. Through the open door, his room looked clear. His room looked all right.

He put a hand out, but the door wouldn't open. Macleod pushed hard, but still nothing. He could feel it bend but not open, and the smoke was coming down thicker now.

Macleod began to choke and cough. He put a hand across his mouth and tried to force the door again. Then his hand went out to the other side. Again, just a shower wall that kept bending. What about in the middle? He pushed, and suddenly the shower door flew open.

Seoras half stood and hunched over, he clambered out of the shower into his small room, but it too was filled with smoke. He could feel the heat of fire burning at him. Macleod stumbled to the open door of his room. He tripped up on something and fell, coming down hard on his shoulder.

'Fire!' he screamed. 'Fire!'

He rolled over, dragging himself away from the door into the shower room. The blaze was strong; the heat pushing him back, forcing him up against the small chest of drawers near his bed. He tried to hide around the edge of them, but the heat was unbearable.

He was screaming now, believing that the fire would take over his room. *Where had it come from? The shower wasn't even electric. It had one of those mixer taps fed by hot and cold water. There was, what, a light? It couldn't have come from the light. Starting a fire like that?*

Macleod thought about how his hand had pushed the shower door in the middle of the extreme heat, and yet it had been cool. He peeked out from behind the chest of drawers and saw a roaring rip of flame lick towards him. He pulled his head back in and screamed, yelling for anyone to come and help.

There was a clatter of feet from outside the door. It must be firemen. Maybe they'd seen. They must have seen. The heat was so strong it must have spread throughout the building. He heard feet coming into the room. He yelled for them, yelled for them to come to where he was, and a face dropped in front of him.

Her name was Amanda. She worked at the home; nineteen years old. She took little to do with the patients, except bring their dinners, maybe help them with the occasional walk, and she cleaned the rooms.

'Mr Macleod,' she said. 'It's okay, Mr Macleod.'

The girl showed a worried face, but then Seoras stopped shaking, put out his hand, and she took it, giving him a smile.

'It's okay. What are you screaming about? There's nothing here. It's okay.'

Slowly, Seoras stood up and looked over to where the shower was. There was no wall of fire. There was no heat in there, blazing out. Instead, he was starting to just feel a little cool, maybe a draft coming through the door onto his wet body.

'Here,' said Amanda, and handed him a towel. Macleod didn't move, so she wrapped it around him.

'Best keep your dignity. There'll be more coming in, in a minute.'

Sure enough, other home workers entered, and once Amanda gave them a nod, they disappeared back out except for one. She was called Ingrid, and she was not a teenager. Ingrid was a woman of possibly forty and looked after the welfare of a lot of patients. Macleod thought she must be a nurse, or at least had some sort of training, but she stood at the door watching the situation and keeping others out of the room.

'Are we feeling okay, Mr Macleod?' asked Ingrid. 'What happened?'

'It was the fire,' said Macleod, shaking his head. 'There was a fire in the shower. There was smoke. I had to get out. It was burning up here.'

'The room's fine. You're hallucinating. It's okay Mr Macleod, these things happen. Amanda, stay here and walk the room with him. In the shower room, let Mr Macleod see the way things really are and see if he needs to get dressed, maybe go for a walk. Have a cup of—whatever, just stay with him for the meantime. I'll check back shortly.'

Amanda took Macleod's hand.

'Do you want me to fetch some clothes out or pyjamas?'

'No' said Macleod. 'We go to the room. I need to see the shower room.'

Amanda helped Macleod across his room and over to where the shower was located through a doorway. The door was open, including the shower door as well, and Macleod could see what he'd seen that morning when he'd stepped into the shower.

Yes, there was a bit of steam, but that was it, and it was dissipating fast. The water was still running though, but the open doors were allowing the steam to flow out. Amanda reached in and switched off the water.

'You okay?'

'Clearly not' said Macleod, but not angrily. He was much more resigned than that. His brain was playing tricks on him. It was driving him nuts. 'I think I'll lie down again.'

'It'll be dinner soon. Best you eat your dinner,' said Amanda. 'These sorts of things on an empty stomach and the brain not getting fed. It's not good. You need to eat.'

'Okay' he said, 'I'll just dress and lie on top of the bed then until dinner, see if I can get a bit of relaxation in.'

Amanda pulled out some clothes for Macleod and after checking he was okay to dress himself, she departed. Macleod dressed, then lay on the bed, his eyes heavy. He must have dozed off possibly for half an hour, but he heard the beep at six o'clock, rolling his feet off the bed and sitting up on it.

Macleod prepared himself for the walk down to dinner. He was discombobulated, unsure of just what was going on. He put his feet into his shoes, sitting just beside the bed, and as he fetched one up to tie it, something flashed across the window. It was a person. They were in grey. They were shifting fast. It was—Macleod shouted. He yelled at the image.

63

'What's the matter, Seoras?' asked Amanda. She walked around to the bed and sat down beside him. She put two hands up on his shoulders. 'It's okay. You've had a rough time. It's okay.'

'There was somebody there,' said Macleod. 'Somebody was there.'

'You had a fire in here as well today. I know it seems very real, but it's not. This is all in your head and you're going to need somebody to get it out of your head. Or maybe the mind will settle itself down, but it'll get dealt with. It'll get sorted. You just need time off and to step back from it, and a bit of help from someone that knows what they're doing.'

Macleod nodded, but he wasn't so convinced. He stood up and, with Amanda's help, walked to the dining area to have his dinner. Beef brisket was on the menu. In fairness, Macleod enjoyed it along with the potatoes and vegetables. A few of the other residents talked to him, but he wasn't for saying much back. He was shaken by what had happened, shaken by the lack of control of his own mind.

After he finished dinner, Macleod walked through into a small lounge area. He sat and watched some rather banal television. It was keeping his mind occupied, though. Following that, he sat with a pack of cards playing Patience. He had no genuine love for the game, but it kept him busy, kept his mind thinking, kept him wondering, kept him alive.

Macleod couldn't go back in his mind, into that place again. He'd suffered enough. He didn't need to keep repeating it.

It was around nine o'clock when Macleod wandered down the corridor to his room. The door was lying open, and he stepped inside and closed it. He turned to the dresser, taking out pyjamas, undressing himself. Macleod then clambered into them, before walking over to the pitcher of water and pouring himself a glass.

He drank a little, worried that if he drank too much before going to bed, he'd end up getting up in the middle of the night, needing the facilities. He always hated that about getting old. Everything always fell apart. Everything stopped working.

Why couldn't you just get something new to replace it? A new bladder in there, something like that. Surely science could do that these days. There must be a pill or something to stop the pee at night.

He gave himself a quick laugh. Happy now that his mind was going somewhere trivial and not brutal. Macleod turned and threw back the sheet on his bed. Sitting underneath was a piece of paper. It was written in black, only a single word, and from his current viewpoint, it was upside down. He reached over and turned it.

Vengeance. That was all it said. Just *vengeance.*

He strode over to the doorway and opened it to look out into the hall. There were a few of the residents walking up and down, but no one else.

'Amanda,' he blurted, looking up and down the hall. 'Amanda.'

She was at the far end of the hall, but she must have heard him, for she made her way toward him. On arrival, he indicated she should come into the room with him.

'I came back from dinner after playing cards. I got changed for bed and threw back the covers. That was there, Amanda. That's not my imagination.'

He looked over at the young girl. She looked down at it and then back at him. 'I didn't write that,' he said. 'I'm not trying to prove anything. That was there.'

65

'Okay,' said Amanda. 'Okay, or maybe you didn't realise you wrote it. Maybe you—'

'I didn't damn well write that,' said Macleod. 'I didn't. The fire in there?' He pointed to the shower. 'Yes, that was this.' He pointed to his head. 'The people I'm seeing maybe, who knows, but that is real and that was in my bed.'

Chapter 09

I t was two in the morning, and Alison Barton was sweating inside her car. It was cool outside, for it had rained slightly and the air was far less muggy than it had been earlier on in the day. The lights of the car swept along the road, illuminating the lush vegetation on either side, and also the occasional wooded areas. Some had been cut down, deforested. Having grown up around here, she knew they would come back, for the landscape changed constantly.

One year, the trees were gone from this side of the hill. Six years later, they were growing back, and another side was stripped of its green glory. Management, they called it. Alison didn't know if that was the right thing to do or not, but she knew that there were probably far more reasons to do that than to do what she had done.

She pulled the car in at the viewpoint on the Struie Road. When they said viewpoint, there was a small plaque showing land features all around, which sat in the middle of an extended parking area beside the road. It looked like one of those refuges off the motorways, or off a dual carriageway; somewhere to stop if you felt overtired or maybe even grab a quick blast of coffee from your flask.

At two in the morning, there were no other cars here, and the view was distinctly different. There was an obvious moon, but not that bright. Yes, you could make out the firth in the distance, a different shade of dark blue. It didn't stand out the same, not with all the other colours having been denied the light.

Stepping out of the car, she felt the cool wind across her. She felt bad, terrible. He'd helped her procure the item in the briefcase, lying in her boot, although he didn't know he was procuring it for her.

Of course, he hadn't brought the case to her. All he'd done was provide details of when people wouldn't be around, and access codes to get in. It wasn't easy to steal something like this. She had to have her wits about her. You had to be on top of your game, but the reward was going to be so great.

She was sick of her lot, sick of running from this man to that man, sick of not being able to settle down because you could be whipped away to some other part of the world. I mean, at the end of the day, it was work, wasn't it? Nothing more, but a type of work. She had several cases inside the car boot. There was a main one. The others, just supplies for it, but when she handed them over and another briefcase came her way, she'd have enough money to run and never look back.

Alison had always been looked down upon. She was a small woman. She'd been a petite girl, but that had made her want to fight. It had made her want to take on the tough guys. That was why she joined up. Why she was in the army. In fairness, she could fight. The average bloke wouldn't stand a chance against her, but she'd also kept that feminine side. There was more than one way to disarm a man. She'd used the other on several occasions to get what she wanted, but she was tired of that.

Noone could offer her a life here, not the life that she wanted, but this money could. Where would she go? People always talked about the likes of Rio, but maybe not. She fancied somewhere that was truly remote.

Or did she? *This was part of the problem,* she thought, *I can do what I want. I can get the money, but do I really know what I want? Still, with the amount of money coming my way, I can check out places. Of course, it'll have to be somewhere without an extradition order, somewhere where if they find me, they can't bring me back from.*

They would not be very forgiving when they realised what she'd done. Still, who cared about that? She'd done time. Six months for striking an officer, back when she was younger. It wasn't really his fault. He had tried to deal with the situation, one where she claimed another soldier had tried to take advantage of her. The other soldier had been sitting with a broken jaw. The officer had got the wrong idea. He listened to the lies and the rumours that she was a bad egg.

When he told her he didn't believe her, she'd lashed out. It had been one punch, but it'd been a good one. It had caught him just under the chin. He'd stumbled backwards, clattered into his desk, and actually rolled across the top of it before falling down the far side. She'd done six months; six months when she'd reevaluated her life and come up with the conclusion that it needed to change, but she needed to change it in a good way. It needed to be about her. Self-interest was the way to go.

Alison looked out into the cool air and took a breath. She'd missed a lot about this place. The wildness. She liked the fresh smell that the dampness gave, especially after a recent

69

rain. Yes, at times, it could get quite fusty if you were stuck somewhere and there hadn't been a breath of air. But out here on the mountainsides, out here, up in the hills, there was a freshness.

She heard the car approaching from some distance off, lights winding their way up the hill towards the viewpoint. She stood waiting for the man to come. He had approached her at first, asking if she could procure certain items for him, and when she said she hadn't done that before on this scale, he'd seemed cold. She'd turned that around over several meetings at which she had dressed rather provocatively. She had got closer to him, under his skin.

Men with money were daft. Men who could splash out because they could see something they'd want. Not like a man with no money. He'd look and think, 'very nice,' and move on. Those with money or power thought they could have it, and if they thought they could, then they would. She'd have to make a note of that when she got the money, make sure common sense stayed with her.

The car pulled up; the lights switched off, and then when the car door opened, the figure inside was illuminated. Alison wasn't dressed so provocatively tonight. One, because he'd struggle to see her properly. Two, if anything went wrong with what she had in the boot, she would need to get away quickly.

'I take it you have it,' said the man, coming out in front of his car towards her.

'I've got that and a whole lot more for you,' she said, walking up to him slowly, making sure she moved those hips. She snaked herself around him, kissing him straight on the lips.

They embraced briefly before he stepped back.

'We won't be able to have pleasure tonight,' he said. 'I'm not hanging around with this stuff. You shouldn't hang around either.'

'It will be the last time we see each other, though,' she said. 'Don't you want to stay for a while? The proper way?'

She saw the man smile, his teeth bared for a moment. He looked her up and down. She'd worn the tight leggings and a T-shirt. He stepped forward, put a hand on her hip, reached down to kiss her again. When he broke off, he said, 'Maybe. Maybe something quick.'

'You say quick, but you'll want more. You'll want to make it last.'

She knew she had him. Hanging on every word. Men were so easy.

Alison strode over to the boot of her car, opened it, and the light inside illuminated three cases. There was the large one containing the item, and two smaller ones.

'I hope it suits you. It's difficult getting a hold of these sorts of things.'

'It's difficult saying goodbye to the amount of money I'm parting with,' said the man, 'but you're worth it.'

'You bet I am,' she said.

He picked up the main case. 'Let's get this bit done,' she said. 'Then we're going to have a bit of fun.'

The man picked up the two smaller cases and the pair of them carried them to his boot. He opened it and put down the two small cases outside of the boot. He lifted a large briefcase out, placed it to one side and then put in the two smaller ones. Alison put the case she was carrying from her boot into his boot.

'You want to count it here?'

'Are you thinking I don't trust you?' she said.

'If you were wise, you wouldn't trust anyone.'

'Well, then,' she said, 'I'll count it. Shall we sit in my car?' she asked.

'No,' the man replied. 'We'll sit in mine. You can count it in there.'

He picked the briefcase up, opened the rear door of his car, and placed the briefcase in the backseat. He flicked a couple of latches and opened it. Alison got in from the other side and stared at the money lit up by the car's interior light. She began flicking through it.

She would not count it all, but it was there, one million. *One million pounds*, she thought. She flipped through it. Three different piles of it. Looking at it, breathing it in. This was freedom. This was going to take her around the world. It was a means to take her to places. She closed the briefcase, stepped out of the car, and rounded it to approach him again.

'So, we put it in your boot?' he said, but she shut the car door.

'Now, let's have a bit of fun.'

'Here?' he said.

'Well, we're not going to go to a hotel with that stuff, are we? Let's have a bit of fun.' She reached down between his legs, grabbing him, smiling and laughing at him before turning and running over to the wall at the viewpoint.

'Out here in the open?' he asked.

'Definitely. I want to be happy with my last view of the place. You're going to make me happy.'

'I thought I made you happy with the briefcase I gave you.'

'This is a different sort of happiness,' she said, and pulled down the leggings. She lifted her T-shirt up and threw it to one side as well. She kicked off her shoes and then stood absolutely bare, looking out from the viewpoint.

'Whenever you're ready,' she said, 'take me to heaven.'

She heard him shuffling over and then he undid his belt. She could hear the clatter of the buckle.

'Shall I bend over?' she said.

'Definitely,' came a voice behind.

Alison bent, her hands grabbing the wall in front of her. She looked down at the view. Beautiful. This was the way to go. This was the way to remember a place.

Suddenly, a belt flew over her head and was pulled tight around her neck. A knee was driven into her back and she fell forward onto the wall, sharp stones cutting up against her face. He was heavy and drove the knee into her back, pushing her against the wall while yanking back the belt. She choked.

She wanted to scream at him, wanted to call him all the names of the day, but instead, she tried desperately to scramble with her arms. Tried to pull herself back up. Her left hand reached the top of the wall. Her right too, and she clawed at it, harder and harder, but then he drove his knee again into her back. She sprawled. He was pulling so tight that she could feel the breath going from her. There was nothing left within, and she slipped down behind the wall. She was even denied that last view of the place she enjoyed so much.

The man kept the choke in place until the body was truly limp. He reached down, checking for a pulse. They'd left the cases, all of them in his car. He turned and picked up her clothing, placing it in his boot inside a plastic bag. He'd have to destroy that once he got somewhere where he can burn it. Maybe he should move her. No, not worth it. He started doing up his belt. She had been useful, very useful, but she was one

73

of them.

She'd come on to him, actually tried to play him. Well, that would never work, would it? He climbed inside his car, flicked on the headlights as he started up the engine. They illuminated the wall and her naked body lying there, her bare buttocks pointing out to him, hands strewn left and right. She was resting in a very awkward position, and he wondered how long it would be before anyone would find her.

If people drove past in the dark, they probably wouldn't notice. After all, who came out this way at night, especially at this time of the morning?

He turned on the engine, spun the wheel and pulled out onto the Struie Road. It had gone well, and he had what he needed.

Chapter 10

Hope McGrath was worried about her friend and so called in on Seoras at the care home before work that morning. She was involved in a murder case, and she knew she wouldn't have much time, but so far, the night had been quiet. Spending an hour or two with Seoras wouldn't be a miss if she could still make it in for close to nine. Besides, Clarissa had said she'd pop in early to the station and pick up anything that came in.

Hope had always worried about working with Clarissa, more so about overseeing her, but the woman was working hard to ease the load. However, there was an underlying uneasiness in Clarissa that bothered Hope. She had come back, persuaded by Jim, or maybe because there was unfinished business. The person who had put Seoras into this care home, after all, was still walking free. Clarissa had done so much to rescue him, but Hope had the feeling that business hadn't been concluded.

Hope parked at the care home and strode in through the front doors to be told that visiting hours were later. She pulled out her warrant card and said she was here to see Seoras Macleod.

'I appreciate that, but the visiting hours are later. Is this to do with an ongoing investigation?'

'Yes,' said Hope. She wasn't sure if it was lying or not. After all, Macleod was at the centre of an ongoing investigation to capture those who had abducted him and killed so many others.

'I have to tell you he's been rather disturbed of late,' said the woman at the desk, 'so please try not to agitate him.'

Hope smiled. How could she agitate Seoras?

Having been told where his room was, she strode down the corridors until she found it. Inside his room, Macleod was still in his pyjamas and dressing gown and just standing up from the edge of the bed. He turned at the sound of her arrival.

'Hope,' he said. 'It is you, isn't it?'

She looked either side of her. 'It's me, all right. Why? What's the matter?'

'I've been seeing things. Been seeing—well, I don't know what I've been seeing. I think I've been seeing things, but some things are—'

'I'm genuinely here. Look,' she said and walked over, put her arms around him, and gave him a kiss on the cheek. 'Don't tell me you've got women in your dreams doing that.'

He gave a little smile, but then she saw the face go back into a state of worry. It was so unlike Seoras. He was calm in all things. Even when things were falling apart, he could still hold it together. He never looked worried like this, as if the world had gone out of control.

'I'm just on my way to breakfast,' he said.

'I haven't got a lot of time,' she said, 'So I'll walk you down there.' She went to take his hand; he pushed her away.

'I'm not an invalid,' he said. I'm just—I'm just—'

'What?' asked Hope.

'I'm just—well, I'm just not right.'

He looked up at her, his eyes almost pleading for her to tell him what was wrong. Hope didn't know. She was no doctor. She was the one who helped him solve crimes.

'When we first met,' said Macleod as they walked through the door, 'you helped me then. You helped me change. You helped me get past her death.'

He was meaning his wife, and Hope remembered the time well. It was awkward because he came from such a different place than Hope did, and in some ways, he despised her. Yet in other ways, he seemed to almost love her. Seoras was a mess when she met him. Here and now, he was a mess again, though of a very different sort.

'If I can do anything, I'll do it,' said Hope. 'We'll start by getting you some breakfast.'

'I see him; see them all the time. I was in the shower and the shower went on fire. It's so real, Hope. It's so real. My mind is—it's—I can't say. It scares me. It truly scares me.'

'It will do,' said Hope. 'Your mind is you. Your mind is what makes you what you are. Such a detective. You see things before I see them. You're cleverer than me in that way.'

'It's true,' he said. 'You're clever enough, but you work differently. A galvaniser of people. You're a more natural leader. You're strong.'

'And you are too,' said Hope. 'I know what they did to you. I know.'

'You weren't there. You didn't have it done to you.' He stopped halfway down the corridor, turned and hugged her. 'I've missed you, though. Do you know what Jane says? You're my work wife.'

Hope stepped back, laughing. 'Your work wife? What does

77

that mean? I get to clean your suits?'

He gave a wry smile. 'No, she's my partner. In all things. There's stuff in work I can't take to her, I protect her from. I've told her, and she knows. You won't take stuff to John. We take it to each other. I need you to understand now.'

'Okay,' said Hope. 'Let's get you eating first. I can spare a wee bit of time.'

They turned and started walking down the corridor again. Suddenly Macleod stopped and pointed.

'What is it, Seoras?'

'Do you see him?'

'Who?'

'The man in the grey habit. The one with the mask. He's got a knife and a whip. He's coming up here. Hope, he's coming at me. Hope!'

'There's nobody there, Seoras.'

'He's coming. He's coming. '

Hope stepped in front of Macleod, between where he was pointing and the far end of the corridor.

'If he comes any further, I'll take him out,' she said, her back to Macleod. 'He's not there.'

Macleod leaned past her, looking down the corridor. There was no one. They turned and walked on down the corridor in silence. Macleod sat down at a breakfast table, and Hope joined him. The woman from the front desk came in and saw Hope with him.

'Excuse me. You don't get to come in here and get him agitated like that. He needs help, he needs treatment. He needs peace and quiet. You can't come in disturbing his breakfast asking him questions.'

Macleod turned and looked up at the woman at the door.

'Do you know who this is?'

'That's the detective inspector,' said the woman. 'She showed me her warrant card when she came in. Said she was going to ask you questions. You need peace and quiet. You need—'

'This is my friend,' said Macleod. 'If I want her here, she'll be here because the rest of you don't damn well listen.'

The woman came over to Macleod. 'You don't get to speak to me like that.'

'You don't get to ignore me. I told you what's going on, and you're not listening. That's why she's here. So damn well leave us alone.'

The woman looked at him, glared at Hope, and then walked away.

'It's not like you to swear so much.'

'Don't start,' said Macleod suddenly. He really was quite edgy.

'They won't believe you. That man wasn't real. You know that.'

'That's not what I'm talking about. Hope,' he said, reaching over and taking her hand in his. 'My mind is playing tricks on me, but other things have happened. I had a note left on my bed, inside the sheets. It said vengeance. This is after I had another flyer dropped for me. I was at the bowls, and I saw a figure. I went outside and there's a flyer there. Vengeance is mine. Fire. The man keeps telling me he's coming with fire. I'm struggling to separate what's going crazy up here, he said pointing to his head, 'with what's happening outside, but that note was real. That note was in my bed. The flyer is real. It's still sitting beside my bed. Something is going on. Something round here.'

'Are you sure?'

79

'Sure? How can I be sure? How can I be damn well sure?' he said, suddenly agitated. 'I stand in the shower, and suddenly it's on fire. I'm going crackers up here. You get that, Hope? I'm going crackers. I dream, and you're in front of me, defending me, saving me. You've got your hair down.'

'What?' said Hope, a little taken aback by the detail.

'You have your hair down. You don't wear your hair down at work. Never do you save me with your hair down.'

He seemed to run away with himself now. Seemed to be…

'Next you're going to tell me I'm wearing some sort of bikini while I do it.'

Macleod stopped and looked up at her. 'It's been a while since I thought of you like that.'

She was always amazed that he could admit to it. Stunned that he didn't just knock that notion away. 'I don't know why your hair is down,' he said. 'Maybe it's because you came as my friend, not as my work wife, whatever that is.'

Macleod leaned back as scrambled eggs, and coffee were put in front of him. The woman who served him went to walk off. He called her back. 'Can you get my friend a coffee too?'

'I'm not supposed to.' The woman was Filipino.

'All I'm asking for is a damn coffee,' said Macleod, but Hope put her hand up.

It's okay. It's fine.'

Macleod looked at her. 'They need to be more reasonable. They need to…'

'She doesn't speak the language that well. Who knows what grief she'll get if she does it? That's not you, Seoras. You would have spotted that. Seen how uncomfortable she was. You're not you.'

'I may not be me, but I've got the feeling, and it's there, and

80

it's still with me. Something is up here, Hope. You know me, what I'm like. You know how I see things, but I need you. I need you to do the spade work, the groundwork, the work that says, actually, he's right. Know it's not just a feeling, or if it's my mind gone bananas.'

'Eat your breakfast,' said Hope. 'You'll need it.'

'You sound like them now. That's the trouble. I'm not making my own decisions. I'm not in charge of me.'

'You're still in charge of me,' said Hope.

'No, I'm not. You'll be temporarily stepping up or someone else will be drafted into the DCI role on a short-term basis until I come back.'

'Well I'm picking up the team and Jim is picking up the paperwork.'

'That's good,' said Macleod. 'You don't realise what a favour he's doing you with that.'

Hope saw him laugh again. It warmed her heart to see it, but then his eyes became fierce.

'I'm not in charge of you, but I need you. I need you to chase this through for me. I'm right with this. I'm right with this, and all I have got is people turning around and telling me I'm not. Chase it through and find me the evidence. Find me what it is I'm seeing.'

'What if you're wrong?'

'Then I'm wrong and you'll tell me I'm wrong because I trust you. I trust you. You know what I'm like. You know how good I can be with this stuff, but you also know how to make it all become clear. Point out the issues with what I'm saying. You can put the evidence in front of me, you can bring me to a rational thought with it. You don't normally have to because this noggin is usually on tip-top form, but at the moment, it's playing tricks on me. Some people I'm seeing are not real. They're in my head.'

'Some?' queried Hope.

'Some, but I think there're others here that aren't in my head. They're real, Hope. I'm scared. I'm terrified.'

'Scared you're losing your mind?'

'Yes, scared I'm losing my mind. If I'm wrong, I'm losing my mind, and that scares me, but the greater fear is if I'm right.'

'What do you mean?' asked Hope.

'If I'm right,' said Macleod, 'he's not finished. He's coming back, and he's talking about vengeance. Vengeance, Hope. You've seen what he's done before. You saw what he did to me. He hanged people and butchered those ministers. He shot Jane, and he shot Angus. I want you to…'

'No need. Clarissa is on that. She's at Clarissa's and Frank's. I'm sure she told you.'

'She did, but Clarissa is…'

'Clarissa is fine. Well, she's not fine,' said Hope, 'but she's of sound mind. She's uneasy about something, but she's sound, and she's thinking straight. She's doing a damn good job. I need her at the moment, and she's coming through.'

'She's uneasy because she hasn't caught him. God love her, she came for me,' said Macleod. 'My Rottweiler.'

'Your Rottweiler,' laughed Hope. 'Do you know what they said at the station?'

'Do I want to know?' said Macleod.

'Macleod's women to the rescue.'

Macleod laughed. 'It's a bit of a change from the older days down in Glasgow. Barely had a woman on the team. Now, I have a secretary. Is Linda helping you?'

'Linda is helping Jim with the admin. Seoras, we are okay. I

82

am here for you. I will look into this, and I will find out, but you need to get better. Give me a moment. I want to talk to someone.'

Macleod ate his scrambled egg while Hope walked up the corridor. She asked the woman at the desk if she could talk to the primary nurse or whoever looked after Macleod. Hope was led through to Ingrid's office, where the woman was sitting behind a desk with a rather dour face. She had big shoulders and looked over a pair of half-moon glasses.

'I don't really talk about patients. There's a confidentiality side to this,' said Ingrid.

'I'm not here about his well-being. Not from the mental side. He says that someone has been in his room. He said that there're pieces of paper with vengeance written on them. Flyers.'

'He's seeing things. He's hallucinating from the trauma he's been through.'

'What about the paper?'

The woman pulled it out of a desk drawer and placed it on the desk in front of Hope. She looked at it.

'It doesn't look like Seoras's writing.'

'The mind can produce what it wants. He's seeing things. There's nobody been through here. It's difficult to get in. It's difficult to work your way into a patient's room. You come through the front. We see you.'

'Do you have CCTV?' asked Hope.

'On the outside. We tend not to use it in the rooms. We're about all the time, anyway.'

'I'd like to take that CCTV over the last couple of days, just so we can run through it.'

'If it makes you feel better,' said Ingrid, 'but trust me, this is all

83

in the mind, and we will get him there. He'll go for treatment soon. He'll have a specialist. They'll sort him. I know you're his colleague and you care for him.'

You have no idea, thought Hope. She smiled at the woman and thanked her and returned to the dining room where Macleod was just finishing his eggs.

'Seoras, before I go, I've got one thing to ask you.' She pulled out her pad from inside her jacket, and put it down in front of her. 'That's a Gaelic word,' she said to Macleod. 'What's it say?'

Macleod stared at it. 'Are you sure that's the spelling?'

'It's Gaelic. I come from Glasgow. Of course, I'm not sure of the spelling. Why? What is it?'

'Salachair. It means dirt,' he said. 'We would have used it to mean "whore" or something akin to that in English. I guess that's the English translation. It's incredibly derogatory. Why are you asking?'

'Got a suspect that said it. Called someone it. Someone he was going to potentially use and then kill. At least that's what I think.'

'He's probably from the Western Isles, or his family is from Lewis or Harris. That's what we would have used back home.'

Hope thanked Macleod, gave him a hug, and stood up and went to walk out of the dining room. As she did so, Macleod shouted after her. 'Hope, that's where he said it started. That's where he said I sinned. That's the core of this. Is it not? Too many connections.'

'Yes,' said Hope. 'I'll get there. You get better.'

She turned and walked up the corridor, back to the front door of the care home. Her mind chewed over what had gone on. As she did so, her mobile rang.

Chapter 11

Hope left the care Home in a hurry, taking her car out to the Struie Road and the viewpoint towards the Dornoch firth. Clarissa called her, advising of the death of a naked woman and a car left behind with nothing in it. Hope made her way as quick as she could. When she turned up, she saw the road closed and parked just outside the cordon before being let in by a uniformed constable. Up ahead was a pair of tartan trews and a shawl that she recognised. She called ahead.

'Clarissa, what's the deal?'

Clarissa turned around from staring at a part of the ground.

'Boss,' Clarissa replied. It must be serious, reckoned Hope. She's using the term boss.

'Jona's just looking at the body. I've cordoned off quite a bit of the scene. If we go over to the wagon and get the outfits on, I'm sure we can go up. We've had some pictures taken. Ross has gone back to the base to work out what's going on. Got Susan with me. Left Patterson in the office keeping everything moving.'

'Do we know how she was killed?'

'I believe it's strangulation, but Jona's looking to confirm.'

'Nice place to die,' said Hope.

'Not at the time that she would've died. I reckon that the murder would've taken place in the middle of the night. It would get dark up here. There are no street lights, nothing. Strange place for you to meet though, isn't it? Unless it's illicit, if you're doing something that you shouldn't be.'

'What do you mean?' asked Hope.

'We've got a car here, and she's dead. There's nothing in that car. There are no other cars here. We can't find any tyre tracks, but then again, it was wet, and that's now dried up. They were careful not to skid to a halt, leave any tread. There's nothing in that sense. Why come up here? Why be naked? Susan thinks it's a serial killer leaving the naked women, but that makes little sense when we include Banner. Why is Banner dead? He took stuff.'

'Let's get a good look at her,' said Hope, and walked with Clarissa over to the forensic wagon to pick up some coveralls. A couple of minutes later, they approached Jona. She was leaning over the victim.

'No closer till I say,' said Jona.

Hope watched as the woman bent down, looking at the underside of a naked woman. Jona was so professional in her manner that sometimes Hope forgot what she had to do in her job. She was currently lying on her back, looking up at the underside of a dead body. Yet, she was doing it in such a calm fashion, almost as if she was a mechanic checking the underside of a car. When she crawled out from underneath, she smiled over at Hope.

'How was he? I heard you were going over.'

'He's not good,' said Hope quietly. 'He's seeing things. Trauma's coming after him.'

'That's what Jane's been saying. She's worried about him. Thinks he's losing his mind,' said Clarissa.

'There's something else,' Hope said to Clarissa. 'He thinks somebody's about. He thinks there's somebody actually in the home.'

'Has it got him that worked up?'

'I think he might be right,' said Hope. 'He's losing his mind in one sense, but it hasn't changed. It's still incisive. Seoras can still look at the facts around him. He's not living in a mad world. Suffering, yes, but the real world he can still see and act in and understand. He's piecing things together. His problem is nobody there believes him.'

'Your problem is you've got a naked woman sitting at the side of the Struie Road viewpoint, and why is she here? Very few people I know drive up naked in the car,' said Jona. 'To then stand having a good look out at what would be a very dark viewpoint. I put her death between one and four o'clock. She was asphyxiated, strangled by what looks like a belt. Certainly, got the width of a belt. Might get somewhere if any of it has come off on her neck, but it would still be a long shot. It will not help you find the guy, but it might prove his presence if you got the belt, if indeed it's a guy.'

'Something makes you think it's a guy,' said Hope.

'Look at the way she's positioned,' said Clarissa. 'That's a guy.'

Hope looked at how the figure was spread. It wasn't pleasant, but she could see that idea.

'Dominance,' said Clarissa. 'She can't see him. He's killed her without her seeing him. In charge, he's the boss.'

'What about her back?' asked Hope.

'There's bruising. Sure, it's a possibility,' said Jona.

'Did he…?' asked Hope.

'She's not been sexually interfered with," replied Jona. 'No, nothing's touched her below.'

'The other victim who was a prostitute, she wasn't one?'

'No,' said Jona. 'Neither of the women has been sexually interfered with. Our other victim, Banner, he was probably excited at the time, but it doesn't mean he was in the process of copulation.'

'Why strip her naked if you're not going to act upon it?' asked Hope. 'Why kill her in the first place? She must have come up here to meet him. You don't come up here to hang out. Same with the Falls of Shin. You don't go to the Falls of Shin in the middle of the night, especially as a woman. You'd be vulnerable, open to whatever creep came along.'

'Oh, by the way, I think this woman can handle herself as well,' said Jona. 'She's got toned muscle.'

'Really?' said Hope.

'Very much so,' said Jona. 'She's strong. That might be why she's in that position, although how to get her into that position, you'd have to be very strong to do that forcefully.'

'She knew him,' said Clarissa. 'We're suggesting that she knew a guy and she actually, what? Went into a position for him?'

'It's not the craziest suggestion,' said Hope. 'Makes a lot of sense. She wouldn't see the belt coming either.'

'Maybe he's had sex with her before. Any way you could trace him from that?' asked Clarissa.

'It's unlikely,' said Jona. 'Very unlikely. She'd have washed everything since then. If he had done the act tonight, we'd have had a good chance of identifying him through DNA and that, but he didn't.'

'Does that mean he's someone who could be identified by DNA? Is he clever enough not to leave any behind? Is he wary of it?'

Hope turned away. 'Why meet here?' she asked. 'I mean, we are all ladies. You've got a man you like. Are there many men who'd suggest to you, "Let's go up to the Struie viewpoint. Let's get it on up there in the middle of the night outside of the car?"'

'It's a bit of a leap, isn't it?'

'I can get the coming up here,' said Clarissa. 'I can get getting away from everybody if they're just going to have sex, but in the car. Why here? Of course, if he means to kill her…'

'Let's assume,' said Hope, 'let's assume that this is a similar killing to the Falls of Shin. Now Susan's jumping towards the serial killer. Why? There's a woman, and she's left naked. Banner doesn't come into that. Why is he dead? We haven't got consistency in method. Well, what we have got consistency in is people coming to a place that's remote. We know Banner gave away documents. Was something brought here for an exchange. We need to know who this person is. We need to know quick.'

'Well, you got the photographs. You can see if anybody's missing,' said Jona. 'I'm sure someone would miss her. I'll see if there's a DNA match from her.'

Hope walked away and left Jona to her work. Clarissa followed her.

'How is he? Really, how is he?'

'He's not good. He seriously isn't good,' said Hope. 'The problem we've got is he's like us. It's unfinished business. I think if he knew the guy was put away, he might be able to start to heal, but I'm no expert. I'm not a shrink. He needs

89

to work through all that. What's bothering me is he might be right about the other side.'

'Someone being in the care home? Do we need to get some officers around?'

'I've got some CCTV footage I want Ross to go through and see if anything's there. Trying to prove that somebody is about won't be easy. Also, if we jump on it and the person is about, they might start reacting differently. Seoras has an incisive mind. It's still there, even though it's troubled. I think he's being logical in what he's saying. He's trying to work it out and trying to prove it. But if I take this to Jim, I think he'll think Seoras is nuts.'

'You need to stick by him, though,' said Clarissa.

'Indeed, we do. Anyway, finish up here and we'll get back to the office. We need to find out who did this as well.'

Hope's phone rang, and she picked it up, walking away from the rest of the contingent.

'Ross, it's Hope. What have you got?'

'The dead woman. I think I know who she is.'

'Who?'

'Alison Barton. Military.'

'Well, that explains something. Jona said she had a muscular physique.'

'She's also in a bit of trouble. I think she may have stolen army weapons. She's down as an absconded army captain. I've only spoken briefly to those in the military, but they were very keen to talk about getting her back.'

'Do we know what she stole?'

'No, but I have some people for you to talk to. The military base is quite close, up near the Tain range. I believe she's had a few problems in the past. They said that it wasn't beyond belief that she'd try to get away from it all. I'll let you talk to them directly. You'll get better information that way.'

'Very good. I've got some video footage I need you to look at for me,' said Hope.

'From where?'

'From the home.'

'Why?' asked Ross.

'Because the boss thinks he's being watched, being messed about with. He thinks our killer's tormenting him. Trouble is, he's seeing him in his mind as well, in visions and in a lot of other places that he shouldn't. I don't believe the boss is completely crackers. The mind's still there and he's getting through it. I think he's realising that something is up.'

'Whatever. We need to catch him. I mean, after what he did to the boss last time. Do you want me to get a detail sent over?'

'No. I want you to look at the CCTV I've got for you. I'll be back at the office soon. Check for people in grey habits with masks on walking about, but more than that. Check for who is about. When you get the images, get down to the care home and see if you can work out who's who and who shouldn't be there. There may be visitors, of course. It will not be a straightforward task, but I think it's suited to your efforts.'

'Okay,' said Ross. 'Will do. Anything for the boss.'

'How are your arrangements with Angus? Is he secure?'

'We've still got people at the house. Angus thinks it's overkill, but I'm not happy leaving him. Not at the moment.'

'I wouldn't be. Good,' she said. 'Make sure they stay tight on that. Clarissa is looking after Jane.'

Hope closed the call and then noticed Clarissa looking at her.

'What?' asked Clarissa.

91

'Alison Barton, absconded army captain. Evidently likes to have some nookie at scenic spots at night. She's also believed to have taken stolen army weapons.'

'VVIP whereabouts and ship movements taken from Banner,' said Clarissa, raising an eyebrow. 'Got a weapon now from this one.'

'Seoras has got a piece of paper that says vengeance on it,' said Hope. 'I'm not so sure our boss is losing his mind at all. He might be one of the few still holding on to his. Come on. We've got an army base to visit.'

Chapter 12

Hope left her car for Susan Cunningham to take back to the station and jumped in Clarissa's little green sports car. Together, the two of them headed over to the military base close to Tain. They would try to find out some more details on Alison Barton and exactly what sort of life she'd led prior to its termination on the Struie Road. The car whizzed this way and that, and Hope felt the wind race across her in the open top. Clarissa would always have the top down whenever she could. The rain was just about holding off as they approached the military base.

'She seems all right. Seoras got her fixed up well.' Hope admired the little car even if she didn't want to drive it.

'Seoras was trying to lure me back,' said Clarissa. 'That's what this was. He never liked this car. He never liked me driving him anywhere.'

'I don't think Ross does either,' said Hope. 'I've got to be honest, personally, I'd drive something bigger, maybe with a bit more punch.'

Clarissa put her foot down on the accelerator and the car hammered along the road. It wasn't a straight track, but the car hugged the bends of the road as if it was on some sort of slot racing track unable to deviate from the centre.

'There's plenty of punch in this,' said Clarissa, finally slowing the vehicle down. 'You know what your problem is?'

'Problem?' said Hope. 'What is my problem?'

'Yes, your problem. You keep that hair tied up. Car like this, you let your hair out. Let it go, especially someone like you at your age. Your hair is still manageable, still does what you want it to do. Take the hair tie off, let it fly out the back. Sometimes you've got to let go even during work, have a bit of style about you.'

Hope frowned. She had style. She had her boots and jeans and leather jacket. Her style could turn a man's head. She wasn't this reckless, rambunctious woman upsetting all the applecarts. *No*, thought Hope, *that's unfair*. Clarissa was not reckless, but definitely rambunctious.

'So did it work?' asked Hope. 'Did the car bring you back then?'

'We've unfinished business,' said Clarissa. 'I came back for two reasons. One, Jim said that if I didn't, he couldn't make his cover story, that I'd been undercover and only he'd known about it. That kind of forced my hand but also Seoras isn't safe yet, we didn't get that guy. What they did to him was horrible and they may come back. I don't trust the fact that they're still out there. They came back before, after the ministers, when it looked like that was that. Whoever is behind this, we need to find him.'

'But when we rounded up the rest of them, they tried to point to that figure. He kept so much from them, even the descriptions they gave us. He was always wearing a mask.'

'Strongly built though,' said Clarissa. 'I can still see the machete, and besides, called me an old woman. It was this old woman that saved Seoras's life, this old woman that kicked everything up to find him.'

'Do you know something?' asked Hope. 'He always said to me I could learn a lot from you.'

'Well, he was right,' said Clarissa.

'And you know why he said that?'

'Because you're too by the book, you don't know when to go off-piste, you don't know what they say is important. If the Assistant Chief Constable gave you an order, you wouldn't know when to break it. You know I envy you.

'Why?' asked Hope.

'Look at you, 6-feet, red hair, trim body. I was decent in my day. I could turn a few heads, but what am I? I'm the Rottweiler.'

'I don't think it's all it's cracked up to be, having a good figure,' said Hope. 'It doesn't help to be 6-feet either. Men don't like you being taller than them.'

'No, they don't,' said Clarissa, 'but I'll tell you something. Seoras doesn't look at you as a woman.'

Hope nearly burst out laughing. 'What do you mean?' she asked.

'He doesn't look at me as a woman either. We're just part of the team. He knew when I went off on my own, he knew it had to be done, he didn't stop me. He came to see me, he came to check if I had lost it completely. But once he saw me, knew I was in control, he didn't stop me. There was no saving the poor female. That probably saved his life.'

'No probably about it,' said Hope.

'And that's what I'm saying. You need to know when to cross the line you need to lead, Hope. You found it hard when I came in, the two of us as DS, and you've got this experienced woman who doesn't take kindly to orders, seems to snap back at your boss. Well, you need to do more of that, you need to bring Seoras into line at times. You also need to learn when to fight dirty. Don't get me wrong, you wouldn't be where you are today without having talent, but to survive in this world, you need a bit more than that. That's why he said you should learn from me. Well, you probably could do with a bit more tact than me, especially if you ever want to get above Sergeant.'

Hope laughed as the car turned into the entrance to the military base.

Clarissa flashed her warrant card and was told to drive over to the main car park. The building opposite would have someone on the front desk who could get the commander of the base to talk to her. The little green car turned quite a few heads before they parked up.

Together, they walked into the main building surrounded by many people in military uniform, and Hope thought most of the women looked in good shape. She wondered how Clarissa felt because here she was the oldest. She definitely looked strange by comparison. Then again, if you wore that outfit every day of your life, you certainly couldn't be taking too much heed of what other people thought of you.

Hope flashed her warrant card at the front desk and after a wait of approximately five minutes, they were taken through to see the base commander. He sat behind a large wooden desk, but stood to welcome them, and had coffee brought through for them.

'In truth, it's sad to see her go, although not good the way she went.'

'What do you mean?' asked Hope.

'To be caught stealing.'

'You didn't catch her though,' said Clarissa.

'No, she absconded. You see, Alison had problems in the past. There's at least three men on this base I know she had affairs with. Three men that she broke up families over.'

'Any of those men still on the base?'

'Two of them,' said the commander.

'Can we speak to them?' asked Hope.

'Of course, if you think it'll help, but when I spoke to them, they were just idiots. One thing about her, though, was she could handle herself. Strong, robust woman, but she had that, I don't know if you'll understand it, that way of being strong that attracts a man.'

'Especially men in the military,' said Clarissa. Hope flashed a glance at her.

'What?' said Clarissa. 'Strong woman in the military, one that can stand up to them. Oh yes, because a lot of military people, they follow strength.'

'Yes, said the commander, 'you're right, but what we don't like is dishonesty and not following orders.'

'What weapon did she take?' asked Hope.

'I can tell you it was in three cases. I can't release the exact type. You see, it was a new weapon. It's not on the market yet.'

'Now that sounds dangerous,' said Hope. 'Is there anything about it we should know? Is there any way it...'

'I can't speak about it,' said the man.

'Okay, said Hope, 'but it came in three cases. What size roughly?'

The commander detailed the dimensions of the cases. 'Two smaller ones and a large one.'

'They could fit in the boot of a car though, couldn't they?' said Clarissa.

'Very much,' said the commander. 'Why?'

'She was found naked on the Struie Road at a viewpoint. There were no clothes found with her. There was no other car. The Struie Road is some way out for someone to decide to kill someone. They must have met for the stolen weapon. Certainly, a potential draw for the killer.'

'I thought you were chasing someone who was going after prostitutes or women of the night. That's what the papers are saying.'

'Papers say a lot of things. Where do you get your intel from during a war?' asked Hope. 'I hope it's not from the paper. You know they lie.'

The commander gave a wry smile.

'How much is it worth?' asked Clarissa.

'The device that she took, there's no exact cost on it.'

'How difficult was it to get out?' asked Hope.

'Well, she bedded one of the guys who were meant to be looking after it. Managed to retrieve access from him, codes and clearance badge, passwords. She did a proper job on him.'

'That's an awful lot to do for someone. She must have been good,' said Hope.

'You really wouldn't believe it. She had that ability. Hard to feel aggrieved at her, even when she took the damn item away. I'm still feeling sorry for her, wondering how we can bring her back into the fold. I'm old enough to know better than that,' he said.

'Can we speak to these two former lovers on the base?' said Clarissa.

'Certainly,' he said. The man picked up his phone and then sat in silence, waiting until a uniformed soldier came through. He was ordered to take the detectives to the two soldiers they were requiring to speak to, who were now waiting outside in a separate room.

'I thank you for your time, commander,' said Hope. 'I just thought that I could get a bit more detail on the weapon.'

'Sorry,' he said. 'I can't do that. I appreciate why you want it, but I can't do that.'

'Okay,' said Hope. They stepped outside the door of the commander's office and Hope waved Clarissa over. 'Follow the soldier there. Tell him I'll be in shortly.' She picked up her phone and called a number.

'Hello, is that the confidential line into the services?' asked Hope.

'Yes, feel free to speak your message. You don't have to give your name if you don't want to.'

'I'll give my name all right. I'm Detective Inspector Hope McGrath. Tell Anna Hunt I need to speak to her. Tell her that the military is withholding information. Tain base, a weapon stolen. I need to know what it was. I'm being refused such details. Tell her I can't do my job unless I know what I'm dealing with.'

Hope closed down the call and marched into a small room. There were two men sitting down with Clarissa perched across the other side of a table.

'I'm Detective Inspector Hope McGrath, you've already met my colleague, DS Urquhart.' The two men looked rather sheepish.

'I believe you've both had affairs with Alison Barton,' said Clarissa. 'Let's cut to the chase. I want to know what she was like; I want to know how far she could take things, and I want to know what she enjoyed. What would get her involved with a man?'

The first man gave a cough. 'Alison,' he said, 'probably the best I've had in my life. She could drive you crazy. She could play on you every minute of the day. Sexually, she was provocative. That's the polite word, up for anything, probably more accurate. And not just up for anything, it wasn't usually your suggestion. Oh, she liked to push the boundaries,' said the man.

'That's true,' said the second man. Unlike the first man, who was dark, and this man was fair, his blond hair ever so neatly cut. He had a thickset jaw, but as he spoke about Alison Barton, his eyes seemed almost glazed over.

'Alison—Alison could take you to places.'

'I take it she did more than just sex,' said Clarissa. 'I mean, seriously, guys.'

'Well, that's the thing, you see,' said the blond man, 'she kept taking money off me. Nearly made me bankrupt. That's how the wife found out. Alison could keep you happily separate from anyone else. You could conduct an affair with Alison, and you'd know no one would find out. Except that she kept asking for money. And when she'd drained me of money and of probably every bit of will I had left, she moved on. And my wife saw an empty bank account. Some money spent on things that weren't her and it all went to rat.'

'I was the same', said the dark-haired man. 'So was John. He was the one she started with.'

'Which one of you gave away the codes, though?'

'That was me,' said the fair headed one. 'I worked with the new weapon. In fact, it was not long after I'd started with it that Alison made a move towards me.'

'She made a move towards you?' asked Hope. 'You weren't instigating anything, then?'

The man thought for a moment. 'No,' he said, 'I think most people would say that I took the first move, but I didn't. For about two weeks, she kept appearing in front of me. I went into the gym, she'd be there in front of me. She'd always be in a—well, let's say she was making sure her assets were readily on view to me.'

'But you said that most people would think you took the initial step?'

'Yes, except I didn't. When they look back, I was in her apartment, her room, she was never in mine. When it all blew up, I seemed to take the blame for most of it. She moved on. Clearly, she wanted the money. She wanted the lifestyle as well. The money afforded her, but there was another side to it.'

'What?' asked Clarissa.

'She was one of those women that liked sex. I mean, really liked it, wanted it all the time. Most women aren't like that.'

'You're saying she had an abnormal sex drive?' asked Hope.

'Very much,' said the man. His colleague beside him nodded vigorously.

'And she knew how to perform. I admit it, I gave away all the details. That's why I'm facing trouble now, probably rightly so. It's a pity she's dead, though.'

'If I told you she was found up the Struie Road with nothing on looking out to sea, would that surprise you?' The two men looked at each other. 'Clearly not,' said Clarissa.

'She liked the excitement. That was a spot that, well, having compared notes, she liked the view while she was enjoying herself. I think that's the politest way to put it.'

'I see,' said Hope, 'well, that changes things.'

They ran through some more details, mainly finding out

that Alison Barton could mix it with the men when it came to fighting. But there was little beyond that, that would be of any use. When they exited the room and walked down the hallway towards the front door of the base, Hope heard a shout.

'Excuse me, Detective Inspector.' It was the base commander. 'If you'd like to come in a moment, I've got someone on the phone who needs to speak to you.'

Hope turned and followed the commander, with Clarissa in tow. Once inside his office, he closed the door and Hope heard a voice from the speakerphone on his desk.

'Detective Inspector, don't say I don't react quickly. The commander here is about to tell you what he can tell you, which is a lot more than he told you before, but it will not go down in any notes. Am I understood?'

Certainly, Miss Hunt,' said Hope, 'and thank you for your assistance.'

'They killed one of ours,' said Hope, 'and I was just explaining to the commander that they killed one of his, albeit a rogue, so, Commander, if you would.'

The commander explained to Hope that the weapon was a missile launcher, relatively easy to use, and had two missiles accompanying it. The design was classified and if they were to find it, the return of the item would be most appreciated.

'As you can see, Detective Inspector,' said Anna Hunt, 'we're in a bit of a quandary here, and you're probably our best chance of getting this weapon back. Unfortunately, it's tied in with a rather public investigation, so please, everything on the quiet. If you need my help next time, the commander has a phone number on a piece of paper. Use that, not the confidential line.'

'Well, you didn't give me any number to call you. You said you would get a hold of me. Doesn't work when I need you.'

'Indeed,' said Anna, 'just be advised that I'm not on call.'

'Never dream of it,' said Hope, and she turned, taking the piece of paper. Thanking the commander, Hope left. Once they got out to the little green sports car, Clarissa looked over at her.

'You're learning, I'll give you that. You're learning. I'd have been proud of that move.'

Hope smiled. She sat down in the car, reached around the back of her head and undid her hair tie.

'What's this?' asked Clarissa.

'Back to the station. Don't worry, it'll be back on before we arrive, but this sensation of the wind in your hair better be good.'

'It's better at speed though,' said Clarissa, and spun the wheel, taking the green car out of the car park.

Chapter 13

Jane crept in through the door and then threw her arms around Macleod, hugging him tightly. He nearly rolled backwards from his sitting position on the bed, where he'd been looking out the window. She kissed him gently on the side of the head before holding him tight again.

'How you doing?' she whispered. 'Any better?'

She relaxed her arms, and he sat back up. Jane walked round the bed to sit beside him. She took his hand in hers, for an answer wasn't forthcoming.

'You can tell me, Seoras. Whatever it is, however it is, you can tell me.'

'You didn't see him then?'

'See what?' said Jane.

'The man in the grey outfit. He was here. The mask was at the window. He keeps coming. He keeps coming to the window.'

Jane stood up for a moment, walked to the window, and looked out. She couldn't see anyone. Rain had started, albeit a light drizzle, but it had clearly chased everyone else away.

'I can't see anyone, Seoras. Are you sure you saw him?'

'He was real. I keep telling everyone he was real. Things are real here. I know some things I see aren't. I know at times I'm not seeing what's in front of me, but other times I am, but no one else is. You saw the note.'

'I saw the note,' said Jane.

'They're wrong. I didn't write it. I know I didn't write it.'

'They're saying that you wouldn't know if you wrote it because of the way your mind's been scrambled.'

'I would know, Jane, I truly would know. You see, I've been thinking about this. I haven't got a pen that writes like that. You know me, I can't write like that. I've tried to write like that. Picked out a different pen, and I tried to write like it, but for one, the pen mark didn't come out looking the same, and two, I couldn't form the letters. I can't even copy it,' said Macleod.

'Maybe you did, maybe you didn't. Let's not have a fight. We don't want to go down that route. Let's spend some time together,' said Jane. 'I need my Seoras for a bit.'

He stood up and turned to her, put his arms around her and said, 'That's a good idea. I have enough people telling me I'm mad. Don't need you to do it as well.'

'I don't think you're mad,' said Jane. 'You might be ill, but you're not mad.'

'I'm not ill either,' said Macleod, and then he stopped. 'Well, maybe a little ill. Things do come back at me. I see some things, but other things I'm not seeing. You believe that, don't you?'

'I believe you believe it,' said Jane. 'I don't know what to believe.' He frowned at her. 'Stop that,' she said. 'Stop that. If this was an investigation and you were in my shoes, you would have said what I just said. I have got no evidence to prove, but I haven't got evidence to disprove. Therefore, it's all a possibility, but whatever is, he believes it. And you do, so we'll look for evidence.'

'How do you get evidence?' asked Macleod. 'How do we get any evidence?'

'Well, if you could get a hold of this guy, physically touch him. More than that, bring back something from him.'

'Of course,' said Macleod, 'and that'll be because I'm just the fastest, most lithe person going. Also, I haven't just come through the worst torture I've ever endured in my life, so catching them, that's going to be easy.'

'None of this is going to be easy, Seoras. There's no need to be like that with me. I'm helping you. I'm trying to show you how you prove this.'

'Yes, you are,' he said. 'Sorry, love.' He reached forward and kissed her on the cheek, but she grabbed him and pulled them close, kissing him deeply. When she broke off, she stared into his eyes.

'We will get through this,' she said. 'We will get through this.'

'I know,' he said, but there was a lack of conviction in the voice.

'Let's go for a walk,' said Jane. 'Grab your coat. Come on.'

'But it's drizzling outside. You sure you want to go?'

'Shut up, Seoras, and just get your coat. I want my man. To take him away from everyone else for a half an hour of my life, okay? I want to get out of this place, so you can stop thinking about this damn stranger that keeps wandering in and you can focus on me. I need you,' said Jane. 'Hell, Seoras, I was shot. I nearly died.

'Now, I'm not putting that up against you and saying that what I have was worse than what you got. This is not about comparisons. This is about me needing you the same way you need me, so screw all the investigations and ideas for now. Let's just be the two of us for an hour.'

106

Macleod nodded, turned, and grabbed his coat. She was right. Jane was so often right. That was the thing about her. Normally, she was much more upbeat, but after being shot, something had been taken from her, and with his woes added on to that, Jane was struggling.

'We'll walk down to the beach,' said Macleod.

'Good idea. You don't get many people going down there.'

Macleod took her hand and together they walked out of the front door of the care home, coats on, braving the drizzle. They walked round to the far side of the building, then down the steps that led towards the beach. The view from the care home was spectacular. It was something that Macleod appreciated, but the crunch of the rocky sand underneath his feet was also a blessing.

They trod along the sand, each having to fight as their foot slipped down through small stones and sand, leaving behind small craters. It was hard work, and soon they were puffed out and stopped for a moment. Macleod sat down on a rock and Jane plonked herself on his lap.

'Come here, love,' he said, and he pulled her close before setting his head underneath her chin.

'That's it,' she said. 'That's it. I want to do this some nights, and I can't. You know that. I can't because you're stuck in here.'

'You'll have to come over at night then, and we'll pop down here when no one's about. Run away in a scandalous fashion.' He laughed.

'Now I know that you're not well, talking like that.'

Macleod grinned and held onto her tight as the rain changed from a drizzle to the beginnings of a downpour.

'We're going to get wet,' said Jane.

107

'Don't care,' Macleod said quickly. 'I don't care. As long as you're here.'

Macleod could hear footsteps. There was a crunching of small stones on the move. It was barely audible over the now fast-descending rain, but Macleod, with his detective mind, instantly needed to put a face to the noise. Staring over to the far end of the beach, he saw a man in a monk's habit. The same man. The man he'd seen before.

'Can you see him?' asked Macleod suddenly.

'Where?' asked Jane.

'The end of the beach.'

She peered. 'No glasses on, Seoras,' she said. 'But that's not a blur. Yes, that's a person. Why?'

Macleod pushed Jane off his lap, dropping her straight onto the sand beneath. He was up on his feet and running as hard as he could. Across the rocks his balance was unsteady, and he made such a clatter that the grey-figured person at the far end of the beach turned to see what was happening. As they saw the racing detective, they turned, fleeing.

Macleod had taken a few walks outside of the care home, to make sure he understood the surrounding terrain. It had struck him as the man ran off that if Macleod cut left, up off the beach, and across the grass, he could cut him off close to the large rocks at the end of the beach. It was worth a shot.

'Seoras, where are you going?' called Jane after him. Macleod ignored her, trying to pump his knees hard, driving them up, keeping a pace, but the sandy footfall caused him problems. He scrambled up onto the grass plane.

The man was getting away. He had to get him. Jane said she'd seen him. That meant he was real. This wasn't a figure of his imagination. This person was real!

As he cut across the grass, he could see people at the windows of the care home looking out at him. There was an orderly suddenly running from the building, shouting at him to stop, but Macleod had passed him by. He ran along until he reached rocks at the top, rocks that were high from the beach.

He'd have to clamber down them, slowing him up, but he wasn't sure where his quarry had gone either. Macleod reached the top of the rocks, looked down and saw the man taking off a grey habit and throwing it into a small motorboat. He was about to step in. Macleod had to stop him. The man had to be stopped. He was real!

He glimpsed it. The man was below him now. The opportunity wasn't a sure bet, but if he could…

Macleod ran towards the edge of the rocks and threw himself off, dropping a good eight feet down on top of the man trying to escape in the boat. Macleod didn't tackle him, more just sort of fell onto him. As he hit the ground, Macleod winced in pain, his shoulder impacting the damp sand. He wasn't sure if it was badly damaged or just bruised, but certainly, he had felt better.

The man he'd jumped onto had rolled right to one side and then jumped back on Macleod, who lay on the beach as the man tried to hit him, Macleod's arms waving in front of him.

'Got you,' said Macleod, but felt a punch across the chin. He was shaken this way and that, but he drove a hand upwards and pull at the man's ear.

'Just stay down,' said the man. 'Stay down!'

'No way,' said Macleod. His hand reached up and grabbed the man's hair. He kept pulling at him, time and time again, as the man tried to escape. Macleod felt a punch in the stomach, followed by another one and then one to the jaw and his hand pulled.

Slowly the man was winning the fight, hitting Macleod several times down towards the kidneys before then trying to stand up. He jumped on board the little rowboat that would take him out to the larger vessel. Macleod could hear Jane huffing heartily as she came round the headland and he rolled over onto his back.

The blows to the kidneys had hurt, really hurt. The person obviously knew what they were doing. Jane ran up to him when she saw the obvious pain he was in. Tears filled her face.

'Are you all right,' Seoras, 'Are you okay?'

He looked up at her and grinned. Then she held up a pair of shoes. She had lobbed them off when she had followed him, carrying them in her hands. He laughed at that.

'I'll get my phone,' she said. 'I'll get my phone and call the police because he's getting away, and by the time anybody gets here, that boat could be anywhere. If he comes back, we'll hide in some little nook or cranny.'

'Don't worry,' said Macleod. 'Don't worry.' He was beaming from ear to ear.

'Why?' asked Jane. 'Why should you be happy?'

He unfurled his hand beside her, telling her to look at it. There in the middle of his hand was a snatch of hair.

'DNA,' he said. We've got the DNA. We've got him, Jane. I've got him. Take me to Jona. We need to get this to Jona.' And as the rain pelted down, Macleod laughed heartily in the middle of it all.

Chapter 14

Things had turned on their head and Hope McGrath was worried. She'd been worried before about Macleod's mental state, but this was more frightening. Someone had got close to him. Someone may have been standing at the end of his bed. Was it the man who had previously tortured him? The man who had organised these killings?

It made Macleod a central focus. He'd made Macleod a scapegoat for something Macleod did not know of. Hope had given the hair sample that Macleod had taken from the man and sent it to Jona for analysis. It was something physical, something tangible. Hope thought that it might at least give them some idea of who the man was, or if it was somebody else impersonating him. Some sick joke to play on Macleod. Not that the other joke was all that funny when they took him, beat him and tortured him.

She'd also called in the team. They were at that sticky point of an investigation and Macleod was always keen to pull everyone in to hear what they had to say. Unlike the main briefings, where everyone was invited, these were always a select few, the primary team, and it was a very open forum.

Although he was convalescing, Hope wanted Macleod to be in on the meeting, for he had seen this figure and any questions, any relevant links, might need to be answered or substantiated by Seoras. But she was also confused, because while Seoras was seeing this man, and he had apparently been real, killings had still taken place. To what purpose?

Previously, he'd attacked ministers who had, in a former life, abused others. He also went after companies deemed to have messed around with people's finances. Hope could see a line of attack there, could see a reason. But now she had three dead in her hands: a prostitute, a man from the Secret Service who had been to see that prostitute, and an absconding army officer.

The only tie between the two scenes of killings was the way the women had been left. Everyone had been left with nothing on, but what was the point of that? What was being said? What was being done? It made little sense. If they were going after Macleod, if this person truly wanted Seoras, why kill the others? A list of movements of some very important people had been taken, serious enough that she'd been approached by the Service. And now a weapon had been taken.

The briefing had shown that it wasn't a weapon of unbelievable destruction. This was no nuclear bomb. It certainly could fire missiles, and that meant that the target it could hit was reasonable: a building, maybe a boat, maybe a car, a bus, maybe even an aircraft. Things needed to move on.

Hope pulled her car into the police station car park, strode out up the outside steps, and then the stairs towards the main office. She looked round it and saw the familiar faces of her team before approaching her office. Inside was Ross.

'Are we ready?' asked Hope.

112

'Just about. Usual issue trying to get him sorted with technology. You know what it's like.'

Hope nearly laughed. Macleod was well known for not being the greatest with technology. That's why he had Ross, but his being present in the meeting was important.

'I'll go get some coffee sorted.'

'No,' said Ross. 'I've got someone doing that. I believe you said she was to make the coffee.'

'Oh, yes,' said Hope. 'Yes, apologies for that. Wanted to bring her in. Wanted to…'

'Yes, well, you'll have to drink it,' said Ross. 'I made my own.'

Was that a hint of indignation? Was Ross seriously angry at her for that? Surely not. Hope didn't have time to worry about such trivial things and sat down behind her desk, looking at some of the morning's mail.

'Jona's going to join us, is she?'

'Yes,' said Ross. 'I believe so, but you'll have to give her a bit of time.'

Five minutes later, Ross indicated he was ready, and Hope told him to call the team through. Clarissa, Susan Cunningham, and Ross sat around the small desk at the side of Hope's office with a TV screen behind it. Macleod was sitting in a shirt and tie. Hope realised he'd made an effort. There was no way he was going to sit there in his pyjamas or even a light casual shirt. This was work, after all. She could see he was focused. Something must have been reborn in him. The detective had awoken.

'Oh, we will not wait for Jona,' said Hope. 'We brought everybody in today to see where we are on this case, but first, let's bring everybody up to speed to what's happened to the boss.'

'Not the boss at the moment,' said Macleod. 'Just an old madman in a care home.'

'Fighting for a lock of hair,' said Clarissa. 'What's wrong, dominoes just not enough fun.'

Macleod glared at Clarissa before giving a wry smile.

'That's right,' said Hope. 'Seoras was struggling with seeing things and one thing he saw was one of our monks. He was wearing a grey habit, mask on. But Seoras wasn't sure that he was there, and not just a figment of his imagination. He's been having some hallucinations because of the trauma that he suffered.'

'Some hallucinations,' said Macleod, 'but not this one. Not this one.'

'Why, what happened?' asked Susan.

'I apprehended, well, failed to apprehend a man who was walking around the care home dressed in a habit and with a mask on. After a brief chase, I tackled him on the beach. He got away, but I got a handful of hair.'

'And I've sent that over to Jona. Hopefully, she'll be here soon with some results.'

'Do you think it's him?' asked Clarissa.

'Definitely,' said Macleod.

'Let's not get ahead of ourselves,' said Hope. 'At the moment, we don't know who it is. Hopefully, Jona can find out for us.'

'It's him,' said Macleod. 'I looked into that mask. The shape, the size, the shoulders, everything. It's him.'

'But we don't have conclusive proof, Seoras. Yes, we got a working theory. It's him. But why? Why is he doing this? Why not just grab you? Last time he grabbed you to torture you? Why not do it this time? Why does he have to parade around your care home?'

'Torture of a different sort,' said Clarissa very matter-of-factly. 'He probably knows that Seoras is struggling with his mind at the moment. Maybe he's playing on that.'

'Oh, he's doing a darn good job,' said Macleod.

'Is this tied to the other investigation? The other murders?' asked Hope.

'I don't know all the detail on those,' said Macleod.

'Clarissa, run him through it,' said Hope. She sat down in the chair, tapping a pencil gently on the desk while Clarissa explained all to Macleod.

'Then that weapon's got to be your priority,' said Macleod.

'I know what the priority is, but I also don't know if I've got somebody sick in mind trying to wind you up or if I've got a killer come back again.'

'I tell you now it was him,' said Macleod.

Hope put her hand up towards the screen, praying that Macleod would see it. She knew what he felt, and he might be right. There was certainly the possibility, but he was also extremely compromised in forming a sensible opinion.

'What do we know about our killer?' asked Hope. 'What's our key feature about the killer at the moment?'

'He likes to leave them in the nude,' said Susan. 'Maybe he's got a sexual fetish.'

'Not convinced,' said Hope. 'I'm truly not convinced. I'm thinking this might be his way of trying to cover up. None of the women were sexually abused. Neither was Banner. Why take their clothes?'

'There was the other thing,' said Ross. 'About the Gaelic word.'

'Yes,' said Macleod. 'That's very important. This word means something akin to "whore" in Gaelic, used in that way.

115

It's something we may have used at home if we particularly disliked a woman. Highly derogatory.'

'Could you just have learnt it from someone?' said Ross. 'Would you?'

'No, they wouldn't teach that in that fashion. That's a word that comes from being in amongst the language, from growing up with it. I'm telling you now, your killer, I think he's from home. Lewis or Harris.'

'Well, if he is, I'm not sure how that helps us other than you're from there. Does that mean they're tied in?'

Clarissa gave a cough and then looked round at the others. 'I need to explain something,' she said. Hope raised an eyebrow at her. Then gave a nod, allowing Clarissa to continue.

'I went over to the island after they brought Seoras back. I went to find out if anything happened back in the day.'

'We know it didn't happen. There's nothing on the records,' said Hope. 'We know Seoras did nothing in his time, so it seems a case of fabrication, a weird fantasy.'

'It's an extreme bit of fabrication,' said Ross. 'You don't take the boss and torture him in that way unless, well, you have very strong issues with him.'

'Shut up,' said Clarissa. 'Everybody just shut up for a minute. I went over to Harris, down to the care home where McNeil is living. I had a word with him.'

'You say you had a word?' asked Macleod. 'What sort of word?'

'I went to understand what was going on,' said Clarissa. 'It's why I'm back. It's why I'm here. There's no proof of this, but Mary Smith lived on the island before Seoras was an officer there. But the other officers who received the killer's cards were there. McNeil, Beaton, Henderson and Clark.

'Around that time, Mary Smith came into the station to report that she'd been interfered with by a local minister. McNeil told me they were struggling at the time with a shortage of good ministers. This minister was doing so much good for the church. So McNeil managed to cover it up. None of the others were involved. Just McNeil, who shipped Mary Smith off to the mainland where she got a job and a life. He said that was all fine, and the church went on.'

'What?' said Macleod. 'That can't be right!'

'Yes it is, Seoras.'

'That man lectured me,' said Macleod. 'That man actually questioned my faith, he…'

'Whoa,' said Hope. 'Personal feelings. Let's keep them out. Keep going, Clarissa.'

'Well, the thing was, the reason they've all got sent these cards when the ministers were getting killed, is because our killer believed all the group was involved. And for some reason they've seen you, Seoras, as being the big part of it. Maybe it's because you're the most high profile. People would know your name.'

'But I wasn't there,' said Macleod. 'Never heard of a Mary Smith. I said before I only knew Mairi Smith. Who is Mary Smith? And you said I wasn't there.'

'You weren't, but a Seoras Macleod was; just not you. You came to the station afterwards. The Seoras Macleod that was there lasted eighteen months. Apparently our killer doesn't do his records very well. That's why I came back, because I knew it wouldn't be over.'

'You didn't tell us this,' raged Hope.

'I didn't want it brought up. No doubt McNeil would've denied it all. It was just me there and there were no records.

Wasn't much I could really do. Besides, if sleeping dogs had lain down, I'd have let them lie. Seoras didn't need this, but now our killer's come back. That's different.'

'I want a word with you afterwards,' said Hope, pointing at Clarissa.

'She's done it for the right reasons,' said Macleod over the video link.

'Don't,' said Hope. 'Don't. There was a coverup how long ago, it's ended up with all this because somebody kept something to themselves, so don't, Seoras. Don't. Don't defend her. I know she came to your rescue, and we all thank her for that, but this should have been reported to me. What did McNeil get? He should be hauled up for that.

'I spat in his coffee,' said Clarissa. Hope thought she heard Ross laugh.

'What do we know then?' said Hope. 'He's back. He's got a reason. Even if he's mistaken in his reasoning, we can't exactly send him a note and say, "Oh, by the way, you are looking out the wrong Macleod. You need to go after the other one."'

'He's dead, our other Macleod,' said Clarissa. 'I did think to warn him, just in case he was still around and our killer figured out his mistake.'

'You thought to warn him. It was important enough that you felt he needed warned. Somebody who's been out of the force for however long and the killer isn't actually coming after.'

'I also warned the others.'

'Okay,' said Hope. She was fuming and about to lose it with Clarissa but there were more important things right now. 'We'll talk about that later. Meantime, we've got a weapon missing. We've got very important persons and their movements being broadcast to other people. There's also this hair sample. I'm not convinced yet that these things are connected, but there's a likelihood, maybe a strong possibility, but I don't see the endgame here.'

'The endgame is vengeance,' said Macleod.

'What?' gasped Hope.

'They left a flyer behind. Vengeance is mine. Things on fire. He intends to do something big. He's not simply looking to kill me. If he was, he'd have done it. He was at the end of my bed. Been close to me, and he hasn't physically harmed me. He's locked into a plan. He's going to do something shocking, a statement.'

'I'm going to contact Anna Hunt again,' said Hope. 'Because of the weapon, we may need their help in looking to see who could acquire it. Or if there's been any other rumours about people looking for other weapons. You can't get these weapons or lists on the normal market. These things are tied into the services and the military. I'm going to need her help with that. In the meantime, Ross, see if you can get any information on this Mary Smith. Clarissa, you better help him, seeing as you know so much about it. I take it we've had nothing from the CCTV footage around the care home.'

'He's good,' said Ross. 'Nothing. I do have a list of images, though, in case he's entered without being dressed.

'Susan, liaise with Ross with that. Get those images and get over to that care home. Find out who's a regular visitor, who isn't. Get names to the faces.'

'Will do. That's easy.'

'Right, dismissed then. Get on with it. Seoras, I'll speak to you soon. Stay safe, please.'

The video link went down, and the team began to leave the room.

'Not you,' said Hope over her shoulder. Everyone knew who she meant, and she stood looking out the window until she heard the door click behind.

'What the hell?' asked Hope.

'He didn't need it. He didn't need it. If I had brought it up, you would've kicked off with it and he'd have been brought in to talk about this, talk about that. Macleod needed none of that. Seoras was not well and Seoras needed looked after. I came back in case anything happened; to look after him. It happened; I spoke.'

'You talked to the others, and you never filed it on a piece of paper. If you weren't here in five years' time and it comes back, who knows about it then?'

'I would've said to him when he recovered. Seoras would've known by then. McNeil's got a lot of clout,' said Clarissa. 'He may be in a care home, but he's got a lot of clout, and over there, places will shut down quickly. "No evidence. Nothing. There's Clarissa slandering an old man." I came back here. I knew if it became important, I'd tell what I knew. Look, I hate what McNeil did,' said Clarissa. 'Screwed up big time. It's not right, but he put her out of the situation. He gave her a life somewhere. He didn't just throw her under a bus.'

'Maybe,' said Hope. 'Whatever he did has spawned someone who's prepared to take lives, who's prepared to torment and torture my friend. When this is over, we'll talk about this properly. I can't have a sergeant that holds things back like that from me. Dammit, Clarissa. We are a team.'

'I did it for him. He's had enough. He's got too much on his mind. You would've done it too.'

'No, I wouldn't,' said Hope. 'He knows that as well. There's a reason you're a sergeant. I can see that now. I understand why when we were both sergeants, he made me the lead one. He knows you too well. Yes, he knows your strengths, and he told me to learn from you. But he knows the weakness.'

'Well, if weakness is looking after your friends…'

'Don't you think I would've looked after him, too?'

Clarissa turned around, walked over to the door, opened it, and then stopped.

'Ultimately, no. You'd have put the case before him like he does, before the important things of life. Being intact, being happy. You treat this as if it's a be-all and end all,' said Clarissa. 'You have to win the game. Have to come out the other end understanding what happened and put those people away. There's a bigger picture. Maybe you'll see that one day.'

She turned, walked out, closing the door behind her. Hope just stared, her cheeks as red as the hair in the ponytail behind her head.

Chapter 15

Hope was still seething when she contacted the number that Anna Hunt had given her. A voice on the other end, which had a deep masculine tone to it, advised that Anna would meet her in a coffee shop in Inverness. It was approximately ninety minutes later that Hope made her way down. She had hung on at the police station hoping that Jona would come back with an ID on the hair sample, but so far, the forensic lab had been silent.

Hope wrapped a leather jacket around her as she walked along the streets, the rain beginning. She entered, looked around for Anna Hunt, couldn't see her, and so ordered herself a coffee. She took it and sat down at a table. Five minutes later, a woman in black jeans and a green waterproof jacket entered. She bought herself a coffee and came over and sat down beside Hope without asking.

'Well, this is pleasant, isn't it?' said Anna Hunt.

'I could think of better places. You could always have popped round to my office. I wouldn't have had a problem with you coming in.'

'I would've had a problem being there,' said Anna. 'You guys don't get it, do you? We operate on the quiet. We like to meet in places that are open. There's a good lot of noise here. This café, particularly, it's quite busy, but you can also see who's coming and going easily. Now, I am a busy lady despite the rather casual appearance, so if we could get down to business. Why did you want me?'

'You said you wanted to be kept informed about the investigation? Well, this is me keeping you informed.'

'You could have passed it over the phone,' said Anna, 'unless you want something.'

'This is getting more complicated than you might imagine,' said Hope. She reached round the back of her head and pulled at her ponytail, flicking it this way and that.

'That bad,' said Anna. 'You're about to tell me something and you're worried I won't believe it. Trust me, in my profession, you keep a very open mind. What's the matter?'

'I'm worried that the weapon being stolen may be tied in with Macleod, and the mysterious figure that he's been seeing.'

'He was referred to the care home as I believe,' said Anna Hunt. 'He's been having hallucinations.'

'No, he's been having visits,' said Hope. 'I'm not sure if it's from some sick bastard or if it's the original man who tortured him.'

'Nasty business, that one,' said Anna. 'I hear you found him, managed to save him before they could finish him.'

'My colleague Clarissa Urquhart, she found him.'

'And she wasn't even working for you at that point. That must have sucked,' said Anna. 'Not like your team got there before her. She went and kicked things up, I heard.'

Hope wondered just how much of a watch Anna had been keeping on the team.

'It's not like that. I don't sit and watch over you all the time.

Seoras Macleod is quite a senior figure within the police force, and he gets kidnapped. There were a lot of killings happening to quite important people. Not very, very important people, but important people. I was asked to take a look, to see if we needed to intervene instead.'

'What do you mean, intervene? It was a police matter,' said Hope.

'You have matters,' said Anna. 'This is a police matter. This is a civil matter. We don't have matters. We just have problems, and for certain people, that was becoming a problem. When it was just the ministers, that's just tittle tattle, normal police work. But when it became financial institutions being attacked and then a police officer taken, and given the fact that you'd made no progress on the case, well then we were asked to look at it. But Miss Urquhart took it upon herself to sort it out. Or is she now Mrs Urquhart. Whatever, she did a pretty good job of it as well. That must have hurt you, though. You're a systems person, aren't you?'

'I don't follow,' said Hope.

'You work within the system. Macleod does too, except Macleod's very flexible, very adaptable, and he's got the mind for it too. He's one step ahead of the game. That's what makes him so good. I did, at one point, think about bringing him in for us, but he gave me Kirsten instead. Macleod's not really in a condition to work for us, physically I mean. Kirsten Stewart was much more suitable, and she thinks like him in a way you never did.'

Hope stared at Anna Hunt with narrow eyes.

'Don't be like that,' said Anna. 'We're all different people. The world needs people like you, people that follow procedures and toe the line. Dogged, hardworking, but it also needs the people who can take a matter by the balls and deal with it. Clarissa gets frustrated with normal police work.'

'Be that as it may,' said Hope, 'what I can tell you is that Macleod is the wrong person they've gone after. There was another Seoras Macleod, worked at Stornoway just before our Seoras took over. He's dead now, but Clarissa went to find out what had happened. McNeil, who was the senior officer at the time, admitted to covering up sexual harassment of Mary Smith and shipped her off, all to keep a decent minister there. It was all him, nobody else. So they think Seoras is the man behind it and they're wrong.'

'But people think what they think,' said Anna. 'Why do you think it's...'

'I don't think it. Seoras thinks it. He said they left a leaflet with him, said *Vengeance is mine* on it, showed large explosions. You've got your weapon that's been stolen. You've got very important people. I'm thinking there may be a connection, but I can't prove it yet.

'But Seoras has said it. Macleod has said that he thinks there's one there, and over the years you've learned to trust him, haven't you?'

'Yes,' said Hope.

'Well, I touched, but what do you want from me?'

'Was there anybody else coming looking for this information? Anybody else approached about this VVIP list, or anyone approached about weapons? Do you know?'

'Yes,' said Anna. 'I thought that and I've checked, but no one's come up on the radar. One problem here, I think, is that it's not a figure that normally plays this way. Whoever they are, they can certainly move in the dark. You've seen that with a large group. You couldn't find them. When you all came to him and you rounded them up, you can't find him,' said Anna. Hope looked aggrieved. 'I'm not criticising,' said Anna. 'These are the facts. He clearly can move in the dark. I thought maybe he's a former agent, but I can't find anything.'

'We know he called one prostitute he approached to work for him, who would have been involved in the first killing, "Salachair". It's Scots Gaelic from the Western Isles, in that context.'

Anna Hunt sat forward, looking at Hope. 'So, he knows his Gaelic?'

'No. He's brought up on it,' said Hope. 'That's the thing. He's brought up on it.'

'Where's Mary Smith?' asked Anna.

'I'd thought of that. She's not. No record. I can't find her. She gets shipped off to the mainland. Maybe they changed her name. Maybe they did something else.'

'I don't like this,' said Anna. 'I really don't like this. Normally, even when things are serious, people have form. You can find them in the past.'

'What I was thinking,' said Hope. 'We've got a clutch of hair from the man who was at Seoras' care home. Seoras actually chased him down. Tore it off him.'

'Maybe I underestimated your DCI. Maybe he could have worked for me.'

'I don't think he'd work for you on principle,' said Hope. 'That aside, I'm wondering if our killer's not planning something bigger. That's why I hoped you might be able to dig up someone brushing in, making contacts, trying to get equipment. I just don't get it. He clearly wanted to hurt Seoras. Jane, Macleod's partner, is under Clarissa's protection at the moment. Macleod doesn't have any other family, so where does our killer go? How is he going to to injure him?'

'Maybe it's not him,' said Anna. 'Maybe it's just somewhere associated with him. Got to remember that Macleod takes things personally. He sees himself as a guardian. It's one flaw that we don't like.'

'I hardly see that as a flaw.'

'That's why you don't work in my profession. There' are a lot of flaws. Kirsten was able to iron hers out to a large degree.'

'And how is Kirsten?' asked Hope.

'Not for discussion,' said Anna. 'I'll go back and do a bit more digging, but you continue with your investigation. In this case, I think you might get at this guy quicker than we can. I'll be listening and watching, though,' said Anna. 'And keep me informed.'

'That's a two-way thing,' said Hope. 'I need you to keep me informed, too.'

'Of course. You'll have all the relevant information you need.'

'And you'll decide that? I'm used to getting all the evidence, all the information, making my mind up about what's important.'

'A luxury I can't afford to give you,' said Anna, 'as much as I'd love to. What sort of sandwich do you like?' asked Anna suddenly.

'What?'

'A simple question. What sort of sandwich do you like? They're selling them up there. You can have it in a bap, you can have it in one of those nice slices of bread they've got. I like prawns. Do you like prawns?'

'I like prawns,' said Hope. Anna stood up, went to the counter, bought two prawn sandwiches, and brought them back, placing one in front of Hope.

'Thank you,' said Hope.

'It's on the taxpayers' expenses. You don't have to thank me,' said Anna. 'Can I give you a bit of advice?'

'Advice?'

'Yes,' said Anna. 'You seem very agitated.'

'I am agitated. I've had one of my colleagues hold back information to look after someone else.'

'Yes, and that person would be Clarissa Urquhart, I guess.'

'How did you know?' asked Hope. 'How closely do you watch us?'

'You weren't surprised that she knew me from our first meeting?' asked Anna.

'I thought she might have bumped into you. She said she crossed paths with you in the art world.'

'We did, only I sought her out. We have many experts, but she turned us down. A mistake, in my opinion. Some advice, if I may. If you're going to let people have a free rein to do things, at times they will get it wrong. Trust me, I've seen things go spectacularly wrong by letting people do what they feel they should do. It's a learning curve, even for someone of that age, but it's the best way to be. Don't suffocate them now because you've had this setback. Embrace it and let them learn.'

Hope looked down at her prawn sandwich. 'Why are you telling me this?' she asked. 'Why are you offering this advice?'

'You're a woman on the up. When you get to the top, it's hard to stay there. You think your world's tough. Mine's unbelievable. Just a sister passing on her knowledge,' said Anna. 'Look on the bright side. At worst, you've got a prawn sandwich out of it.'

Chapter 16

Hope returned from her meeting in Inverness to find Jona sitting patiently in her office. She had in front of her a sheet of paper and had plonked herself in a chair straight in front of Hope's desk, even though she wasn't there. The Asian woman was sitting quietly.

Hope opened the door, and Jona didn't turn around. 'Sorry, am I interrupting your meditation? Feel free to borrow my room anytime.'

'You have actually,' said Jona, 'but it's okay. I'll forgive you.'

Hope walked round the desk and dropped into her own chair, and then saw an anxious look on Jona's face.

'What?' said Hope.

'Feeling the pressure a bit? I heard it wasn't a great meeting that I missed.'

'Somebody kept secrets from us.'

'That's the same person who found Seoras. I'd be very careful what you do, especially in front of the team. Clarissa's got very large capital at the moment.'

'I didn't do it in front of the team.'

'Really?' said Jona. 'I thought you did. In truth, I'm amazed it's never come to blows before with you two. You're very

YOU ARE A WEAPON

different. Macleod knew that. That's why he liked the both of you on his team. Very different opinions, unique weapons to use.'

'I'm a weapon to use.'

'It's an accurate analogy. Maybe not the most flattering.'

'What have you got for me?' asked Hope, testily.

'Easy. I knew you were frustrated. Right. I got a positive ID from my hair sample.' Jona saw Hope smile. 'It's from a Norman Greenhalgh. We've got him because he was once arrested for breaking into a jewellery shop in what was back then, a rather poor attempt at robbery. He lived in Aviemore for a while, and I've got a last known address here. I don't know if he's still there, or anything else about him, but that's him. At least it was when he stole the jewellery.' Jona pointed to a photograph at the bottom of the piece of paper she had.

'At least they'll be able to find out if he's just a lunatic, or if he was the real lunatic coming after Seoras.'

'Are you okay?' asked Jona.

'Yes,' said Hope. 'Why do you ask?'

'Seoras is out of action, properly. I heard Jim was assisting you.'

'Jim's taken over the paperwork, so to speak. I'm covering the team, leading the investigations, also looking after the other teams that Seoras deals with.'

'That's not what bothers me,' said Jona.

'Go on then,' said Hope. 'You're going to tell me anyway at some point, aren't you?'

'Seoras is a very different figure. You've taken over a team running as he wants it. Now, when he is there as the boss, that works fine because he's carrying the can and he comes in and he's able to move things about if he sees it. You however, think through things very differently. It makes you, I think, operate differently, and that's quite a jar on the team.'

'And she undercut me. She undercut us all.'

'You are agitated. You know why Macleod has you on the team?' asked Jona.

'And you're going to tell me, aren't you? I've just about had it up to here with people telling me who and what I am, and how I fit into this. Am I having problems at the moment? Am I having difficulties? I've got dead bodies and I've got a boss who's seeing people. More than that, he actually is seeing real people as well. Yes, I'm hacked off, but not as hacked off as I am with the number of people who are coming and telling me how I should be and what the issues are. Frankly, Jona, I wish most of you would just piss off and let me get on with it.'

She saw Jona smile. 'What? What is that for?'

'Good,' said Jona. 'That Hope's coming out. Let it out. Dominate. Take charge. You're an incredibly amenable person. Hope can work with anyone. You don't get up in their face, but sometimes you need to. Clarissa was wrong. She needs to be put back in her cage and there'll be ways and means to do it, but she also did it because she cared.

'You've struggled ever since Macleod moved up and you became the DI. It's like we're still running the same team, except he's not there. He's not doing all this because he has other jobs to do, other functions to run. The last one got so big, and he stepped down and he took over again and we run it the same way. This is your team. The only person whose relationship with you hasn't changed is me because I'm not in the team. I'm the person who slides into the team, but I have my own team. I have my place. Forensics is separate.

'These guys are your people. Ross is getting eggy, getting

annoyed because of what's happened and you're waiting for Macleod to deal with that. Clarissa's gone off on a limb because of what happened. The only person you've got as a blank canvas now is Susan. Patterson's barely working a desk job. You need to lead.'

Hope sat and looked at her Asian friend. She saw the smile. Not a pitying smile. Not an "I know better" smile. Just genuine warm affection.

'Thank you,' said Hope. 'Now you can piss off.' Jona laughed, and Hope followed her to the door.

'Clarissa, here now, please.' Hope sat down behind her desk and Clarissa marched through, shoulders raised.

'Look,' said Hope. 'You did wrong. I'm sorry, but you did wrong and I'm not happy about it, but I need you on this now. Go make amends. Norman Greenhalgh, that's the guy whose hair ended up in Macleod's hands. He lives in Aviemore, or at least the last known address was. Find out who the hell he is. Take Cunningham with you.'

'I can manage myself.'

'No, you can't,' said Hope. 'I've got a killer running around. He's picking on our DCI and he's possibly got weapons with him. You'll take somebody with you as backup and also as a voice. At the moment, everything's running high within us; emotion, tension, desire to get this guy. We need to cover each other off. We need to make sure that we make the right decisions. Take Susan with you.'

'I'll take Ross.'

'No, take Susan with you. One, she needs the exposure to…'

'I need Ross.'

'We're not here to fight. Do what you're good at. Work out who this guy is.'

Hope wasn't sure that went too well, but Clarissa called Cunningham, and together the two women departed for Aviemore. Hope went down to Ross's desk and showed him the information on Norman Greenhalgh.

'Let's search for this guy online. See what you can find about him.'

Hope returned to her desk, sat down, and went to ponder through some files, but stopped and thought. She looked through the windows into the outer office.

'My team. Jona's right,' she said. 'Got to make them my team.' Twenty minutes later, Ross came through.

'Look, this is only preliminary and I'm not saying that I've got everything on him, but from what I can see, a guy with the name Chris Greenhalgh at that address in Aviemore has closed down all his bank accounts. All the money removed. Everything he's published or subscribed to online is gone, wiped. I can try to get some of it back, but that's going to take time. There's only one page left up.'

'Which is?'

'It's a moan about injustices. Given our killer's background with the ministers and then the financial institutions, seems to be consistent, but he goes on for a rant. He doesn't mention the place he's talking about, but he talks about a dwelling at the sea. He talks about a lack of trees.'

'Anything else?'

'And the wind and the peat, but he also mentions it's where a wench was abandoned. Lot of detail on that one. The lady in question is, or at least it suggests, has had improper actions carried out on her, and she's forced to depart. He doesn't talk about a minister, though. He talks about a lord, a laird, but that might just be cover. It's quite vitriolic. Brutal when he

133

calls for vengeance. Time for them all to burn.'

'We've got to find him, then. It's a must, Ross. Weapons. He's taking a weapon with missiles to make people burn, Ross.'

'Yes. I'll get back. I left Patterson working on it, but I've got to be honest, Patterson should be out in the field. He's not a desk guy. Doesn't do the systems the way I do. He doesn't— well, he isn't able to check through. I find that. Get a uniform up here. Some of them are dynamic around the computer. Others should be out there on the street. Patterson's a person who should be out on the street digging the information up out there.'

'Very good. Soon as he's fit enough, we'll get him doing that,' said Hope. 'Anything else?'

Ross shook his head and went to turn away.

'Alan.'

Ross turned back. 'Alan, is it?' he said.

'Yes, Alan, I'm looking for an honest opinion. Do you agree with what Clarissa did?'

'She got him,' said Ross. 'She got him. She got Seoras back. I'm not sure if I wouldn't have done the same in her position, but I had responsibilities at home. When they shot Angus, I just wanted to kill somebody, really kill somebody. If they'd got through to Daniel, I'd have torn them all apart. Was she right to withhold the information? Probably not.

'She was looking after him. I get her comment, letting sleeping dogs lie. Stuff like that. As for the boss benefiting, I don't know. I really don't know. Certainly, I don't agree with doing it in the first place, but you get to a time and place in life and you wonder what's for the best. I don't know. Were you right to have a go at her for doing it? Of course you were. You're the boss. You have to keep the standards, don't you?'

'Thanks, Alan,' said Hope, 'appreciate it.'

'You know she respects you, don't you? You know that having to admit what she did and to come clean about it in front of everyone, especially you, that was hard for her. She's a proud woman in a lot of ways. In terms of years, you were always her junior and yet Macleod put you above her. He very much showed her he thought of you as the leading type, not her. I think it hurts her. She sees herself as capable. She did a lot of leading in the art team.'

'Macleod could always control her. He could always aim her in the right direction, bring her to heel when he needed to.'

'I'm not sure that's the description you're allowed to use these days.'

'I don't give a toss, Alan. She was his Rottweiler and when we were side-by-side as sergeants, that was fine. But I'm the DI now. If she's going to be a Rottweiler, she needs to be my Rottweiler.'

'Yes, she does. Do you think you can live with her being that?' asked Ross.

'Can I live with it? What do you mean?'

'When the two of you were side by side, you were a great team, but now, now one's the boss of the other. If I'm honest, I see friction. I see two very different parts. You're not like the big boss, Hope. You have your way of doing it. Macleod is ridiculously flexible, but he's used to having his troops out there, playing his pawns and his rooks and whatever else he's got. You're not. You like to lead from the front, go out and do it yourself. Maybe that's something to give thought to because if you're doing that, I don't see you and Clarissa lasting together on the same team very long.'

Chapter 17

Clarissa Urquhart drove down the familiar A9 towards Aviemore. She was feeling rough. Maybe she should have told everyone, maybe it was something that she should have even brought to Macleod, but the man was a mess. He needed to get past his demons, not have more things thrown at him. How would you feel if you'd been tortured in a case of mistaken identity? She'd have gone wild, that she knew. Clarissa would've torn the place apart for the people and maybe Macleod would've too. Who can tell when you were put to that limit? He'd been good to her, though. There was a little green sports car that testified to that.

She knew Hope and she were different. Very different. When it came to the crunch, she had been the one who had got him. She had been the one who rescued Macleod. You'd get no thanks for it. Well, you got it from him, but in the long run, you wouldn't get promoted. Too rough, too tough a cookie. Clarissa wasn't a poster girl either.

Hope had it all: six feet tall, long red hair, a body that would attract any man, and a lovely demeanour with it. She wasn't rough and ready like Clarissa, but Clarissa had settled herself on this. She was going to give it all up again, live with Frank.

He'd been so good. They had got married; she was leaving the force. They were going to have time together.

The man was remarkably cultured, she thought. He'd happily sit down with her at night watching the opera on TV, or sit and listen to her talk about various sculptures. That was the thing. At work, she was talked about as being a Rottweiler, some sort of animal. There was more culture in her little finger than in most of that station. She could be classy. She could talk about some of the most beautiful things in this world with knowledge and passion. Instead, she was trailing after people who hacked other people to death.

Sure, the art side of criminality had its own issues. She saw some brutality in it, but not the same. Mostly, it was thefts. Most were keeping stuff to themselves, artworks hoarded in private collections, stolen from here, there, or wherever. The game was much more elegant. Trying to stay two steps ahead, seeing where they'd gone, tracing through where the artwork had arrived, then unveiling it. Nobody destroyed the artwork when you found it. Nobody tried to burn this evidence. You couldn't. Some of these items were so good.

As she turned off into Aviemore, Clarissa realised she was missing it. She'd come along with Macleod knowing what a detective he was, but generally, she'd been battered and bruised. Yes, she'd solved crimes with him, but she'd seen some horrible sights. None worse than the dead children. She'd known there was evil in the world, but the murder squad…, the murder squad was the pits for it.

From people who killed because they'd been betrayed, to people that seemed to kill for the fun of it. This latest one was baffling and looked like they could be extremely deadly with the weapons that had been stolen. Yes, she missed the art world. Things were simpler and there was a touch of class with it. Anyway, she thought, *once we get done with this, we find who's behind Seoras's torment, I'll have paid him back. I'll have found his killer and Seoras will be safe again. My debt will be paid, and I'll move on. I'll run to Frank.*

The address was a rather rundown flat at one end of Aviemore. As she pulled up to it, Clarissa could see eyes peering out from behind curtains. She wondered if it was him, Norman Greenhalgh. Sitting beside her was Susan Cunningham, who had stayed quiet on the drive down. Whether that was because of the fear of Clarissa's driving, or she could just see the mood Clarissa was in, she didn't know. The girl had wisdom from somewhere because Clarissa wasn't for talking. Having stopped, however, Susan began the conversation.

'Eyes at the window. You think that's him?'

'Could be anyone,' said Clarissa. 'We won't know. It makes it look routine. No accusations on the doorstep, because if there is, we want to make sure we're out of the way. We can bring the roughhouse boys in to handle them.'

Clarissa scanned the panel for the different flats in the building, pressed the correct one and a voice answered.

'Hello?'

'Hello, I'm DS Clarissa Urquhart. With me is DC Susan Cunningham. We'd like to speak to you.'

'About what?'

'About someone that lives in this flat or used to live here. We're looking for a Norman Greenhalgh.'

'I'm not Norman Greenhalgh. Greenhalgh, let me think. Ah, Greenhalgh's used to be the ones who lived here.'

'Okay. Do you have a forwarding address at all?' asked Clarissa.

'No,' came the one-word answer. She glanced across at Cunningham.

'I think we need to go inside,' she whispered, taking her finger off the intercom.

'Can we come inside?' asked Susan.

'I'll take it,' whispered Clarissa to her. 'It's okay.'

'Trust me,' said Susan. She half pushed Clarissa to one side. Clarissa realised Susan was now standing in front of the small camera that was used by the residence to see who was pressing their flat intercom.

'Apologies for disturbing you. Would it be possible to come up?' asked Susan.

Clarissa noted that Susan's jacket had come off, and she was standing in a tight T-shirt. Her hair was also down. She never wore it down when she was working.

'Right. Well, I suppose I could. Are you both coming up?'

'I think that's probably safest, isn't it?' said Susan. Out of view of the camera, Clarissa was nodding profusely.

There was a buzz. Clarissa opened the door and the pair of them stepped inside.

'You better lead the way,' said Clarissa. 'Jacket off, hair down. You are shameless.'

'I don't have your experience or your ability to kick a place in,' said Susan. 'Not yet. Got to use what we can.'

As Susan climbed the stairs in front of her, Clarissa felt an admiration for her colleague. She was right. Of course, you worked it whatever way you could. Clarissa called her shameless, but what had she done except look pretty? She hadn't gone beyond any line of sexuality. She'd just read the man and read him correctly. There was nothing wrong with using your pretty face. Back in the day, Clarissa would have

139

used her face and charm. These days, it was just charm, she thought. Did Frank think it that way? She smiled at the thought of Frank.

They reached the flat door, which was already open, and a man was standing there. 'Do you want to come in?' he said to Susan.

'Thank you,' she said, and the man almost followed in right behind Susan and cut off Clarissa. But then he was aware of what he was doing. 'Sorry,' he said, 'come on in.'

Clarissa took a chair separate from the sofa and Susan sat down right beside where the man had clearly been. He had coffee on the table in front of him, a couple of magazines open.

'Can I get you coffee or a drink?' he said.

'Coffee's fine,' said Susan. 'We don't drink on duty.' He turned and made for the kitchen and Susan shouted after him, 'Clarissa will have one as well. Thank you.'

He'd forgotten about me already, she thought. Then caught a mischievous grin from Cunningham. *The girl's a player,'* she thought, *but then again, that was her reputation in the station, wasn't it? How many guys had she been with? It couldn't have been that many. She certainly knew how to attract them.*

The man made several coffees, came back, placed them in front of them and then sat down attentively, looking at Susan Cunningham. Clarissa sat back and let Susan run the interview.

'Do you know if he owned the flat before you?' she said.

'The Greenhalghs. It was a young man and his mom. I remember because it was a really tragic story. The mom, she was a troubled soul. At least some neighbours say haunted by demons, but she wouldn't speak of it.

'Not at all?' asked Susan.

'Well, Jim, Jim's on the bottom floor. Jim said that she had mentioned a little trouble in her past when she was younger. She came from the islands. I'm not sure he ever said which one, but apparently the reason she came over here to the mainland was that some guy had acted inappropriately.'

'Inappropriately?' asked Susan. 'In what way?'

'Well, some guy tried to have his way with her. That's what Jim said. I mean, that was back in the day. Not like now. Now it would all be blowing up and whoever it was would be hauled in by your lot.'

'And quite rightly so,' said Susan.

'Indeed,' said the man. 'But back then, back then, it wasn't, was it? Whatever happened, she'd come away with it. Jim said it was like a trauma to her. It never left her.'

'When she came over, did she have the boy with her or the man? The young man?'

'No, no. Annie, now Annie's two down from me here. Annie says that the kid was born while she was here, although she went away for a while. I think there were rumours at the time that she was going to get rid of it, but she didn't. She said she couldn't. God would judge her. She might have been right with that.'

'I think God will be more likely to judge the person who put the child in there,' said Susan.

'Well, that too,' said to man, 'but I'm not religious. I'm just telling you what was said.'

'This may be a little forward, sir, but was there anything left behind in the house? Was there anything remaining of their property?'

'Nothing of note. Most of it was binned. I didn't see any pictures or any diaries or anything like that, if that's what you're thinking.'

'Why did she sell the house? Do you know?'

'She didn't sell it. He sold it. He was fairly young, I think, at the time. Possibly sixteen. Maybe fifteen. As Annie tells it, he came home to find her, well, hanging.'

'She committed suicide?'

'Indeed,' the man said. 'You see, according to Annie—and I think Jim, Jim was of this opinion as well—she was ashamed of what had been done to her. Had come away, leaving everybody she really knew and arrived here. She'd gone through difficult times. I know that after having the child, she'd tried some relationships later on. But I guess after a trauma like that, maybe you can't be normal in a relationship. It's a really sad story.'

'And what happened to the young lad?'

'I don't know. I really don't know,' said the man, 'where do you go? Maybe he was fostered. Maybe you guys would know. I never really asked the question. You could try Jim and Annie, but I'm not sure they would know either. House gets sold. Child moved on. He was still young, so I think he might have gone to a foster family. That's what would happen, wouldn't it?'

'Is that just a guess?' asked Susan.

'Very much so,' said the man. 'Sorry, I'm just trying to help you out here. Can you tell me why you're looking for them?'

'I can tell you it's got nothing to do with you and this house. This is just an address we had. Did you have a forwarding address then?'

'Nothing. Not even for the mail. Not even their solicitor. Everything just stopped.'

Susan turned and gave a nod to Clarissa, who nodded back,

indicating that there were no more questions.

'Well, thank you for your help,' said Susan. 'Can I just give you my personal thanks?'

'You wouldn't have a card or something, would you? With your number on it? Just in case I thought of something else.'

'Just phone Inverness Station. Ask for DC Susan Cunningham, if you have any more information.' Susan smiled at the man, then left for the door, Clarissa following her.

As they descended the stairs, Clarissa turned to Susan.

'Good job,' she said. 'Very good job. He would've called if you had given him your card.'

'Absolutely. I mean, it's so easy. Men like that, they don't even hide it.'

'Well, we're back up the road then,' said Clarissa. 'If she committed suicide, there'll be police records. We need to dig that out, see where the young man went, and then we'll see if we can find this guy.'

'You're feeling a bit sorrier for him, aren't you? Now you see what happened to his mum.

'If it's him,' said Clarissa.

'If it's him,' said Susan. But you felt sorry for him, don't you?

'No,' said Clarissa. She could still see Macleod's tortured body. Absolutely not.

Chapter 18

Macleod was pondering what to do. There'd been a greater security presence at the home. He had seen that there'd been activity to identify people from CCTV. Those who had been about the home and whether they were putting costumes on and scaring Macleod and then taking them off again. He felt frustrated, felt trapped. Yes, he'd been there at the meeting where they'd decided what to do. He'd even thrown his tuppence in, but at the end of the day, Hope was running the investigation.

Macleod wondered how she would've taken the fact that Clarissa had held information. He understood it. He really did. Macleod had struggled to come to terms with why someone had done what they'd done to him. He had done nothing wrong, but to know now it was a mistake, to know now he had suffered all that in error, a rage built up in Macleod every time he thought about it. It just wasn't fair. It wasn't. He had told them.

Jane had arrived earlier and suggested she take him out. He asked where, and she said back to the house. She hadn't been there for a bit and neither had he. They'd bought the house on the Black Isle as a place to find quiet and solitude. Maybe that's where they should head. Macleod had agreed, and now, as soon as he had done up his tie, he was ready to go with her. She came into the room.

'You don't have to look so formal.'

'It's not my formal tie. I never wore this tie to work.'

Jane smiled. 'You're looking better today,' she said.

'I'm not feeling it. It was unfair. Do you know that?'

'Of course, it was unfair,' she said. 'I know that, you know that. With these people you've been dealing with, people you always deal with, they're never fair. It's not the point, is it?'

Jane took his hand and when he went to speak to say more, she put a finger up to his lips. 'How about today we just spend a bit of time with each other? Don't talk business, talk nothing. In fact, let's try to not talk. Let's just try to be in each other's company.'

'I'll try,' he said,

'And I mean, be in my company,' said Jane. 'I don't want silence with that brain whirring away in the background, trying to work out what's going on. Just because you're not saying anything to me, doesn't mean you don't get to give me attention. I might run off with somebody else.'

She turned to walk out the door and from behind her, Macleod grabbed her, arms around her waist, and pulled her in tight. 'And I'll reel you back in,' he said. 'I'll hang on to you.'

'Promises,' said Jane. Macleod reached with his lips for the side of her neck, kissed her there, then kissed her ear, and then held her again. 'No words,' he said, 'No words.'

Jane drove the car back up to their house on what had turned into a rather beautiful day. As she turned into the drive and parked, Macleod could see a solemness on her. She was staring over at the front door.

'Come on,' he said, 'We need to do this.'

'Yes, we do. They're not taking my home away from me. This is yours and mine. Always going to be yours and mine. This is where we started our life together. This is where I want to die, in your arms,' she said.

'Little melodramatic,' he whispered.

'Even so,' she said. 'You know what I mean.' He did.

Stepping out of the car, they walked hand in hand across the last bit of the drive and stood up on the stone pavings that led to the front door. Macleod took out a key, opened the door, and pushed it open. He took Jane's hand and together they stepped inside the front door.

She spun. Macleod thought her legs were going to go from under her. He reached and held her, and then she steadied herself.

'It's all right,' she said, 'It's just this is... this is where I was shot. He just came in there, right in front of me. Bang. That was it.'

'We got lucky,' said Macleod. 'We got really lucky.'

Jane turned around, threw her arms around him.

'Then let's ride that luck. Come on.'

She kissed him on the lips, shut the door, and then dragged him through the house. She found a bottle of wine sitting somewhere near the back of a cupboard and she took out two glasses. There was a bottle of mineral water in the fridge, so she took that as well, and the pair of them stepped out to the rear of the house.

There was a small patio feature that allowed them to look out onto the Moray Firth. Jane put the glasses down, as well as the wine and the water bottle. She cracked the wine open. As she poured a wine for herself, she turned to Macleod to ask him if he wanted anything else, but the man was transfixed.

'Can't you see it?' Macleod said.

'No. I'll get your water then, Seoras, shall I?'

Macleod didn't respond. Jane looked at him and saw that he was far off, and then his hand shot up in front of him. 'No, no, no,' he said. Then he dropped to his knees. She watched as, almost unbelievably, he seemed to react to an invisible whip. Jane ran and flung her arms around him.

'Seoras, it's fine. Love, it's just a nightmare. Seoras, Seoras!'

He snapped out of it with a start. She pressed him close to him.

'It's okay, Seoras. It's fine. They haven't got you. You're with me. I have you. I have you safe.'

Macleod was helped up off his knees, but when he looked down, his beige trousers were now covered with a mucky stain across the knees. He turned to leave, and she asked where he was going.

'I'm going to change these, wipe away that episode, and just sit with you. Give me a moment.'

'Are you sure?' asked Jane.

'Absolutely, there'll be trousers upstairs. They didn't empty the wardrobe when I went into the care home.'

Macleod made his way off the patio and up the stairs of the house, aware that Jane was watching him. He felt tired and a little sore. He put it down to the jump off the rocks he'd done previously, bringing his assailant down and grabbing his hair. It'd taken a lot more out of him than he'd thought. Maybe he just wasn't feeling well. The torture had caused it. Or maybe he was just getting old.

In front of the full-length mirror in his bedroom, Macleod stripped down. He decided he'd have a look for something a little more jovial than a shirt and tie because now he was home, he was feeling more relaxed. He went to open the door of the wardrobe on which the mirror was situated and stopped as he saw himself. The scars were deep. In the home, he didn't have a full-length mirror. He knew some of the other rooms had them, and maybe this was their way of protecting him against the horror of the physical trauma. He twisted and turned, examining his back, and was amazed at the number of marks that were still there.

Surely, they would heal, surely, they would go away. He reached forward and pulled open the door of the wardrobe. There was a range of trousers inside, and he picked a beige pair before looking in the drawers beside the wardrobe and pulling out a polo shirt. That would make her happy. Dressed down Seoras; Jane would like that.

When he'd gone abroad, she had talked to him about shorts, but he wasn't quite ready for that yet. Instead, he'd worn slacks like these as well as the polo shirt and she'd smiled. He liked nothing more in this life than when Jane smiled. It was infectious. It worked even on him. Grumpy, as they called him at work. Even Grumpy could smile when Jane smiled.

He dressed and then stood looking in the mirror. He looked all right, didn't he? With all the scars covered, he looked all right except for the face. 'My goodness, Seoras,' he said to himself, 'you look so gaunt.' And he did. He looked pale and pasty. No wonder she was worried about him. He went to turn and leave the room when his eyes spotted the bed.

Jane was one of these people that made the bed every morning. Macleod did as well, except Jane made it to a meticulous standard. You couldn't see whether someone had actually slept in the bed when Jane made it. When Macleod made it, it looked like a half-baked man's effort.

He noted the sheet had been disturbed. Macleod walked up closer to the corner that looked wrong. It wasn't tucked in underneath. Jane would've tucked it in underneath. Whether it had been her previous life's training or whatever, she operated like it was a hospital. The bed was tucked in so well to a standard where it was hard to pull it back out. The sheets almost seemed like one with the bed. There was a showpiece rather than a bed to be entered.

His side wasn't tucked all the way in. It was tucked, but not as far as Jane would tuck it. Macleod walked round to the other side of the bed that was tucked in. He walked back again, took the corner of the sheet and he pulled it back off the bed. There, sitting on the bed, was a piece of paper that wasn't a note. He picked it up, staring at it. It was an involved and detailed piece of work. It told a tale, but in it, Macleod thought the characters were not real. They were allegories for someone or something. He went back downstairs, out onto the patio, and sat down beside Jane.

'What's that?' she asked.

'I've just found it in the bed.'

'Is that why you're holding it at the corner and not properly?'

'I'm not sure.'

He studied it. It told the tale of a woman who was wronged by someone, but she managed to buy two little loaves. One loaf grew up to be big and strong, while the other loaf was always in the dark. The one that grew up to be big and strong sought those who had wronged the woman and then lit a fire under their house.

Jane had listened while Macleod spoke the words aloud.

'Oh God, what's that about? That was in our bed, that

means...'

'They've been here as well. It wouldn't have been difficult. You weren't here. There's not really a watch on the building because we're not in. They obviously couldn't get to you at Clarissa's or they were scared to.'

'Could they be here now?' asked Jane.

'If they were here now, and they wanted to harm us, they'd have done it by now,' said Macleod. 'And if they wanted to harm us, why would you leave a note? This isn't a note that explains anything to anyone else. It's just an apocryphal tale of how someone's going to set alight those who have done wrong to his mother and a loaf at that, a bread roll. They're really going to think I'm crackers when I do this,' said Macleod, 'Reporting a bread roll on fire.'

'Call it in,' she said. 'You better call it in.'

Macleod held up his hand. 'I'm not seeing anyone. There are no illusions coming to me. I am not having some time with my partner screwed over because somebody's come in and given me a note. Everything they do tries to knock me off. Here,' he said, and he tapped his thigh with his hand.

Jane got up off her seat, came over, and sat on his knee. She embraced his head, taking it to her bosom as they held each other tight. When they broke away again, he looked up at her and caught her weary-faced at first, before she turned it into a smile when she saw him looking.

'Seoras, you are going to be all right. You will be all right. You're not mad.'

'Not mad,' he said. 'But I still do see people. It's going to take time, but I will be okay, but more than that, I'll bring these people to justice.'

Chapter 19

Hope raced through the Inverness streets, across the Kessock Bridge, and onto the Black Isle, straight to Macleod's house. The thought that someone had been there disturbed her more and more as she drove. The personal vendetta against Macleod had come to a great fruition when they kidnapped him, but now, someone was there ahead of him. Someone was in the places he loved.

How long had they been there? Was it done well in advance or was it just a chance opportunity, or had they been followed? Was somebody creeping around at the time? Someone had been there at the care home.

Hope parked the car in Macleod's driveway, jumped out, and strode over to the front door. She knocked loudly and heard the cars from Uniform she'd requested, arriving behind her. Macleod was at the door in no time with Jane beside him, and Hope couldn't decide who looked more bothered by this turn of events.

'Didn't you hear anyone while they were here?' asked Hope.

'Heard no one, saw no one,' said Macleod, 'but they've been in, they've been…'

'This is my home,' said Jane, and Hope could see the tears

beginning in her eyes. 'They shot me here. As if that's not enough, then they come and leave things here. This is home. This is our refuge. Our retreat. This is what I picked. You can see the firth out of the back. It's a place to unwind. I brought him here to try to…'

'I know,' said Hope, 'and I'm sorry for it'.

Jane turned and grabbed hold of Macleod, burying her head into his shoulder. He gave Hope a grimace before two constables turned up behind her.

'Do you want to stay with the constables for a moment?' Hope asked Jane. 'It's just I need to take Seoras and have a few words about some things. It's maybe best if you don't discuss them.'

'You can say what you want in front of me,' she said.

'No, Hope can't,' said Macleod. 'You two,' he said pointing to the constables, 'what's your names?'

'PC McKinley and this is PC Adams.'

'What's your first names?' said Macleod, almost sighing as he asked.

'I'm Jim, this is David.'

'Well, Jim and David, this is Jane, my partner. I need you to take excellent care of her while Hope and I have a look around the house. In fact, why don't you come through and see if you can make a cup of tea in the back.'

'I don't need a cup of tea,' said Jane suddenly. 'Don't need to be mollycoddled. I just need this bastard put away.'

For a moment, everyone stood still, Macleod standing in shock. Jane certainly swore more than he did, but she didn't refer to people like that.

'I'm sure we'll get them,' said one constable.

'I'm the Detective Chief Inspector's partner,' said Jane. 'You don't have to do that. You can talk to me like a normal person.'

'Lads,' said Hope, 'go and put the kettle on. Jane, really, go through, have a cup of tea. You're frustrated, that's a medical opinion. You're tense, you're hyped up, you're stressed, you're panicked, you're worried, cup of tea. Sit down. The two lads will protect you.'

Jane looked up at Macleod. He gave a nod and a faint smile at her. She turned and followed both constables down to the kitchen. Soon they heard her explaining where the tea and coffee-making facilities were.

'You think he's been here much earlier? You think he was around?' asked Hope.

'I heard nothing. It was just a case of finding it, you know. You might want to check over the message. Get Ross onto it.'

'I don't understand this,' said Hope. 'Previously, he made his move. He killed people who he thought had done wrong, and that was that.'

'Well, he thinks I've done wrong.'

'But you haven't. Do you think we should put that to him?'

'How?' asked Macleod. 'We just go to the news and, "Oh, by the way, police statement, Macleod wasn't there. It was the other Macleod." How are we going to tell him?'

'Just offering suggestions,' said Hope. 'Who else has been in the bedroom?'

'Just me,' said Macleod.

'Well, let's keep it that way. I'll get Jona over. See if he's left anything behind. Given the way he's been operating, I don't think that's a problem for him. He doesn't seem to leave anything behind. Besides, it's probably this Norman Greenhalgh person.'

'I'm not so sure,' said Macleod.

153

'You think it's someone else?'

'If he's been there, if this is the person I'm seeing all the time,' said Macleod, 'and it's not just my mind playing tricks, it's too much for one person. I think there might be two.'

'He's worked with accomplices before,' said Hope.

'That'd be reasonable. There's no point you guys staying, Hope. 'In fact, you're only going to get in the way when Jona gets here.'

'I don't want to pull Jane out. I don't want to get her to run away,' said Macleod. 'This is our home. Jane's spooked enough as it is, but if we just desperately up sticks and run out of here, she's going to…'

'The key thing at the moment, Seoras, is to keep you both safe. Given the way these people act, given how they've killed before, I'm not happy. I'm not convinced we're able to protect you.'

'What sort of protection do you think I need?'

'I don't know. It's strange, isn't it?' said Hope. 'If it was a mob coming after you, if there was some specific person we could focus on, we could protect you much easier. But this is just some figure out there.'

'I'll talk to Jane,' said Macleod, 'and get her back to Clarissa's. Get some protection around her. She seems to like Frank. He's been quite a steady influence during all this. He doesn't get excited. Very steady, level-headed man. Good job. He's got Clarissa now.'

Macleod's dry sense of humour hadn't left, and for that, Hope was grateful. There was a knock at the door behind her, and she turned.

'Boss. Boss,' said Susan Cunningham. 'Where do you want me to start?'

154

'Not here,' said Hope. 'I want you to take the Detective Chief Inspector back to his care home.'

'Seoras,' said Macleod. 'I'm going to drop my partner off at Clarissa's on the way. Okay, Susan?'

Susan Cunningham gave a nod. 'I'm at the car as soon as you need me,' she said.

'Susan,' said Hope, 'when you get back to the care home, have a look around. Just make sure nobody's hanging about.'

'Of course,' she said and disappeared.

Macleod took Hope upstairs. She stood carefully at the door of the bedroom, looking over to where the note was.

'There's nothing obvious,' said Hope, looking around. 'I'll let Jona deal with that. At least he doesn't seem to be willing to kill you. He appears to have some other sort of hurt in mind. Something you'll be part of.'

'What? And then kill me afterwards,' said Macleod.

'The weapons he's taken, if indeed it's been him, it's quite serious,' said Hope.

'How serious?'

'Terrorist incident, serious. Got Anna Hunt on the case. She wouldn't give much away, but she's thinking it's not normal terrorism. She's struggling because this seems to have come in from the cold. Whoever he is, he's clever. He's not leaving anything to chance.'

Macleod found Jane and took her over to Susan Cunningham's car. They dropped around to Clarissa's first, where Frank was in the garden. When he saw her approach and saw Jane's tears, he stepped forward, and Jane hugged him tightly.

After Jane had calmed down somewhat and gone inside the house, Frank turned to Macleod.

'Should I be worried?' he asked.

'About?' asked Macleod.

'About people coming to the house.'

'We've got a watch on this one. We'll keep a watch on it.'

'Nonetheless, I've got my shotgun in the back. I won't be afraid to use it.'

'Be careful with how you use it,' said Macleod.

'Indeed,' said Susan Cunningham. 'Probably best if you don't.'

'That will be enough, Constable,' said Macleod. 'I'm sure Frank knows his business.'

Susan stared at Macleod for a moment, then gave a nod and disappeared back to the car.

'If anybody comes near,' said Macleod, 'you blow their brains out.'

'Don't worry,' said Frank, 'I've heard the full degree from Clarissa. Nobody's going to get to your woman. Not through either of us.'

Macleod put his hand out, and Frank took it and shook it.

'Thank you,' he said. 'You've got a tough woman in Clarissa. A good woman, but a tough woman. I know she's only here because of me. She really should be back with you and you both enjoying retirement.'

'I'm not sure she's ready for retirement yet,' said Frank. 'For me, I'm not ready for it yet either. Don't worry about us. We'll be fine.'

Macleod thanked the man again and turned back to Susan Cunningham's car. As he sat inside, he could see her itching to ask him something.

'Don't,' said Macleod. 'Don't ask me. I know we're meant to tell people not to use guns. People who use guns and who aren't trained to use guns often end up killing the wrong people or making an absolute mess. I know this, DC Cunningham, and if it was anybody else in there protecting someone other than my Jane, I would tell them that. However, that's my Jane, and this person we're up against is shrewd and nasty.'

'So, what did you tell him?' asked Susan.

'I told him to blow their brains out if they come near Jane.'

'Sounds fair enough,' said Susan. She put the foot down, driving off to the care home. On arrival, Macleod went to wave Susan Cunningham off, but she told them that Hope had said she had to stay there. She was to check out the building and all around it to see if anyone was hanging about. Macleod, however, wandered on down to his room, and when he got inside, sat down on the bed's edge. He pushed off his shoes and gave it an almighty stretch.

As he took off the jacket he was wearing to hang it up, something was bothering him. He looked about; things had been on the move. The place wasn't trashed; it was just the items had moved.

He's good, thought Macleod, after a knot had come to his stomach. *Very good. He's showing me he can enter my places, showing me he isn't afraid to come into my world. While we're up there finding his note, he's down here planting something else. The room has been interfered with, simply moved about'* thought Macleod. *Just here and there. Nothing overdramatic.*

He continued looking around the room, then noted that the bed sheet hadn't been folded correctly, or rather, it had. It had been disturbed, though. He reached forward and pulled back the cover, throwing it right back on the sofa. He saw letters. The name Mary Smith was written in bold marker pen. He stared for a moment, looking down at it, but the only thing that came to mind was, *I don't know Mary Smith. Mairi only.*

157

He continued to stare for a moment until he heard footsteps approaching his door. There was a knock.

'Are you okay, Inspector?' said a voice. It was Susan Cunningham.

'I was just getting ready to… Susan, look at this,' he said. She walked around the side of the bed, stared down.

'Mary Smith, you still don't know who she is?'

'I do not know who she is. Like I keep telling everyone, I didn't know a Mary Smith. Mairi, yes, but Mary Smith who disappeared off had nothing to do with me.'

'Maybe not, but it's got everything to do with our killer. He's not happy about what happened to her.'

'That's understandable,' said Macleod. 'But the least he can do is get the right people.'

'Maybe you're just the most popular person to go after, after all. If he thinks you did it, he might think that the others did it. Why not go after them? They haven't got the profile that you have.'

'This is why you don't want to be famous,' said Macleod. 'Did you see anybody outside?'

'No,' said Cunningham. She dialled a number into her phone.

'Who are you calling?'

'The boss. Hope needs to know about this. I'm also going to get you some extra protection.'

As she was calling to organise more officers to come stand guard around Macleod, he went to the window and looked outside. There was no hooded figure. There was no one in masks, and yet, the letters were already in his bed. Muscles in the back of Macleod's neck flared. He could feel the stress coming on. This was going to end one way or another, and he didn't like the way it was going.

Chapter 20

I t was a blustery night, and she could hear the trees occasionally creak in the wind. The leaves rustled, but all this was good. After all, it was like her favourite novel, *Wuthering Heights*. It was all bleak and windy. She wouldn't be bothered if the rain started down either. Isla was that sort of woman. She liked the outdoors. She liked to feel alive. It had been a strange one though, she thought.

She had never quite seen herself coming to fall for somebody like this, but fall she had. In her line of work, she met many men prepared to take risks. Many men who liked to live a certain lifestyle; one of danger, and one with plenty of money. This guy, though, he had been different, and she'd never expected it to take off.

He'd been asking about bombs and devices, personal ones, ones that could take people out . He'd bought other things off her, other merchandise, the occasional gun, handcuffs, manacles, whatever. There were lots of different things. Over the last while, she'd seen him go through many changes. At first, he was calm about everything. More recently, he'd got more excitable.

The plus side of that was he was more of a raging beast. Yes, that was the way to describe him, wasn't it? Angrier at times, but for that, their close moments had become more exciting. He also didn't have a problem with meeting in quiet places, away from everyone.

He had told her that his name was Andrew, but that was a lie. She could tell easily enough, but she didn't care. Andrew was giving her money, or rather, he was paying for the equipment she was supplying. Equipment that as an arms dealer she could get hold of. Many people were very formal about what they did, but when she had realised she'd liked him and she'd made advances towards him, he had responded.

She was a woman with an acquired taste, a woman that liked a bit of adventure in her love life. He had responded to her with that. One costume he wore was a grey habit. He'd introduced it not long after there'd been those ministers on television, and she thought that was part of his act. When he put it on, he went sullen, acted as if she needed to be punished. Fortunately, Isla was a woman who liked games.

She saw the lights approach of a car but remained within the undergrowth until she saw him get out. He looked around for a moment, then came over towards her car. Isla stepped out.

'Andrew,' she said, taking a few quick steps toward him and flinging her arms around him. She kissed him hard on the lips, but he wasn't responding like he normally did.

'Are you okay?' she said. 'You seem a little agitated.'

'Have you got it?' he said.

'Of course, I've got it,' she said. 'I've never let you down, have I? It's in the boot but come here a minute.'

She placed her hands on his backside, grabbing his rump tightly. Normally, this would send shockwaves off within him, but today he seemed extremely cold.

'What's the matter?' she said. 'We can go somewhere afterwards if you want if out here's too public, if it's too…'

'Where's the bomb?' he said. 'I need the device.'

'It's better to leave it in my car for the minute,' she said. 'You're going to want to take it and put it somewhere safe.'

'Yes,' he said. 'I want to take it somewhere safe.' She noticed him looking around him again.

'Are you okay?' she said. 'Really, you're worrying me now.'

'You're worried about me?' he said. 'You don't need to worry about me. Just look after yourself. Right, come on, where's the bomb?'

Reluctantly, she turned towards her own car and flipped open the boot.

'That's it there.'

'Take it out quickly,' he said, 'on the ground to have a look at it.'

'You just don't do things quickly with stuff like this,' she said. 'It's not primed, it's not set. It shouldn't go wrong, but you do nothing quickly with it. Okay?'

'Okay,' he said.

She reached in and cautiously lifted the briefcase, keeping it level, taking it then all the way to the ground behind the car. She flipped the catches, opened the lid, and inside was this small and compact vest bomb.

'All I've got to do is set up the timing for you, if that's what you want. Or there's the manual switch.'

'I'll be fine on that,' he said. 'Close it up, get it into the car.'

'Okay,' she said. 'There's no need to be like that, though. Do you know how hard it was to get this?'

'I know,' he said. 'I appreciate what you've done. We'll have the money shortly.'

She laid the briefcase gently inside the new boot and then walked away slowly. Isla looked at him again. He was checking the entrance to the car park.

'Nobody's going to be here,' she said. 'There's no one coming. We're alone.' She took the zip of her jacket. It was only a fleece, but it had been necessary while standing there, because the wind was a cool one. She now looked at her lover standing before her and started unzipping the fleece. When it got to the bottom, she let the fleece jacket drop to the ground. She saw him staring at her.

Isla reached down, pulled the T-shirt up right over her head, and threw it on the ground. He barely flinched, but he was looking at her. Good, she thought, and unhooked her bra and let it fall to the ground.

'Our business is done. Let's have some fun,' she said. She stepped forward, and he went to embrace her. Then he saw some car headlights behind him.

'What's that?' he said.

'They'll disappear,' she said. 'I won't, though. Don't want your money. I want a lot more than that from you.'

He reached forward and pulled her close, wrapping her up in his embrace. She reached up, kissed his neck and then the side of his cheek. Then her hands went to roam around him. She noticed that his head was turned back away from her.

Isla reached up with her left hand, pulling his head back and planting a deep kiss on his lips. As soon as she'd finished, he turned back again. He suddenly spun her around, grabbed her from behind, holding her tight with an arm across the throat.

'That's better,' said Isla. 'That's better. Time for a bit of fun then. Time for a bit of...'

In the left corner of her eye, she saw his other hand arrive by her head. It was holding something that caught the moonlight. There was a glint of metal. As the knife came across her throat, she felt herself gurgle, and then she was dropped to the ground. There was nothing more after that.

Scene break, scene break, scene break.

Anna Hunt had lost him. She'd been tailing this woman for so long, but now she'd lost her and was having to double back. There were several turnoffs. That was the problem with the Highlands; at night, everything was so dark, and there were turnoffs you couldn't see because there were no lights. There was just constant darkness. On a blustery night like this, she wouldn't even hear half of what was going on out there.

She drove back again, wondering just where the woman had got to. Isla Bishop was an arms dealer. An arms dealer who seemed to do a lot of dealing at the moment. She was smart, if a woman with some rather bizarre tastes both in her men and also in her lifestyle. Whereas a lot of other arms dealers were living it up here, there, whatever, she was much more than happy to be stuck out in the woods.

There was a glint of light through the trees. *In there somewhere*, thought Anna. She let the car continue to roll on for a bit, then turned it around and came back towards the opening.

She wasn't happy with herself. How had she lost the car? How had she got sidetracked by that idiot coming out of the junction? She'd check if this was it. Of course it could just have been a flash of light, but having nothing else to go on, it was always going to be worth checking out.

Anna turned onto a narrow road with trees on either side. There were no lights up ahead, and as her beams turned across a sign, she saw there was a car park.

Anna killed her lights. She stole up slowly in the car. There were two figures. Anna stopped the car, looking at the two figures in the car park. They were embracing. They could have been anyone. Then the woman was turned around. It was hard to see in the dark. Anna reckoned they were still together for a moment, but then there was a sudden movement in the black.

Did she just fall to the ground?

Anna opened the car door and tried to listen. The wind was covering up whatever was going on. She was still a fair distance away, so she stole up quickly on the edge of the undergrowth. As she got closer, a light flew on in one car, and someone raced away. She looked for the number plate, but it was too quick and side on to her.

Given the headlights from the car racing past her, she couldn't even see the figure that was inside. Anna raced over to where she thought the woman had dropped. Taking out a torch, she shone it on the ground. There was Isla Bishop.

Anna reached down, pulled her face towards her, and then saw that the cut across the neck had been rather brutal. The woman was still warm, but she was very dead. Anna stood up, went to the car of the woman, and after two minutes was able to break into the boot. There was nothing there, nothing.

Anna went back to the woman, trying to see if she had anything on her. It may show who she was there to meet. There was nothing.

Anna Hunt would say she'd never felt anxiety but stuck out here with the wind howling, she certainly felt a little spooked. She did not know if there was anyone further in the surrounding undergrowth. She took out her phone and placed a call to the Inverness police station.

'Can I speak to Detective Inspector Hope McGrath?' she asked and waited while a call was patched through.

'Yes?'

'This is your friend,' said Anna Hunt. 'I've been trying to track down where the supply of weapons has been coming to your guy. I've done it, but unfortunately, it appears that your guy might have terminated that arrangement.'

'Where are you?' asked Hope. 'Do you need an ambulance?'

'Only need to take the body away. It's got beyond any chance of saving this one.'

'We'll be up shortly. Stay there. We need to talk.'

'I think so,' said Anna. 'Isla Bishop was an excellent operator. That's the dead woman. She wouldn't have trusted him, whoever this was, unless she really did. I think you've got a big problem, Detective Inspector.'

She closed down the call, after passing location details, and stood there in the darkness beside the body of Isla Bishop. Rather than continuing to stand, Anna knelt and looked down over the woman she'd been tailing.

The woman was bare from the waist up. There were no signs of marks, cuts, or anything on the torso, just simply on the neck. Had she trusted him that much? Really? She knew Isla Bishop had a tendency for wild things, but, even so, this seemed...

Anna remained there, feeling the surrounding cold. She realised the cold wasn't coming from the night. It was because of what had just been taken. 'Blast it,' said Anna.

165

Chapter 21

Ross turned the car into the car park where the latest body had been found. Sitting beside him in the passenger seat, Hope felt tired. It was all relentless, and she didn't have Seoras' help. She truly felt for the first time she was taking charge of something major, something that affected the boss. The stress was taking its toll on her, but like always, you had to go on; you had to keep pushing, had to keep your chin up. She laughed at herself. *Incredibly British thing to say*, she thought, *especially for a lass from Glasgow*.

The scene before her was a hive of activity, and she spotted the forensic van of Jona Nakamura. However, off to one side was a woman who wasn't rushing about, instead she was standing looking up into the morning sky. It was then that Hope noticed one constable approach her and hand over a coffee cup and a small white cardboard box. From within, the woman pulled out a roll and devoured it hungrily.

'Pull over there, Ross. I'm going to see her first.'

'Who's that?' he asked.

'That's our informant. That's Anna Hunt. She's with the Service.'

'Does she know anything about Kirsten?' he said.

'She'll know all about Kirsten, but she won't tell you,' said Hope. 'I've already tried that.'

With the car halted, Hope stepped out and walked over to the woman, who barely acknowledged her presence. Only when the last bit of roll had been placed in her mouth and a slug of coffee followed it, did she turn.

'Detective Inspector.'

'Miss Hunt, I take it you didn't just happen upon this incident?'

'Of course,' said Anna. 'I think we've got a bigger problem on our hands than before.'

'Why?' asked Hope, wondering how it wasn't big enough already.

'I've been tailing an arms dealer named Isla Bishop. Isla's quite the dealer, but she's someone who loses her head easily with men.'

'She will not lose much anymore,' said Hope.

'Indeed, no. When I arrived, there were two of them. I wasn't close enough before he drove off and I didn't realise immediately that he'd killed her. Looking back on it, he took a knife across the throat.'

'Well, that's not unusual for this guy, is it?'

'What is maybe more unusual is she's half dressed. She was in an intimate moment with him, I think, before he killed her. Hard to see, like I say. When I got up close, she didn't die with the face of someone in terror or fear. It was quick.'

'What's he done it for this time? Is there anything in her car?'

'Unfortunately, no. It seems he's wiser than most of us. He made the exchange before seeing if she wanted to do any extras.'

'Well,' said Hope, 'I wonder what he got away with this time.'

'I'll tell you what he got away with this time. He got away with a suicide vest.'

Hope suddenly felt a chill come across her. A suicide vest? She was used to murders. She was used to people doing bad things to other people. But the idea of killing yourself, to go out intending to blow everybody up wasn't one that she'd come across. Most people had an anger at someone else, had a reason for disposing of them, but to dispose of yourself as well?

'So now he has a detailed itinerary of where people are going to be, but also has a method of firing from a distance, and now of getting up close. I feel there's an attack planned, but they're not sure how to do it yet.'

'You're more the expert in that field than me,' said Hope. 'I see Jona is working on the car over there. Has she given you any detail?'

'I spoke to her earlier,' said Anna. 'She's very coy, though. I had to drop your name.'

'Well, we are all sharing information,' said Hope.

'We need to get a move on this,' said Anna. 'It's coming to a head.'

'Seoras is getting left notes. There was a message in his home. I'll send it over to you,' said Hope. 'But everywhere he goes now, they seem to be ahead of him. Tormenting him by leaving messages like a game, like they're ready to play. Like they want him to know it's all there for him to solve before they do it.'

Anna took another slug of her coffee and then walked. Hope followed, more because she didn't know what the woman was doing, rather than through any sign she was to follow. Soon, it was clear Anna Hunt wanted a little more privacy.

'Macleod,' said Anna Hunt, 'you reckon he did nothing in

the past? You reckon this is all a mistake?'

'Oh, it's not a simple mistake,' said Hope. 'Mary Smith certainly had her troubles with a vicar back then, and things were covered up. It's just that Macleod wasn't the *Macleod* who was there. Seoras came along slightly later.'

'Yet they want to make a show of him. The other Macleod wasn't a major player. Was he?'

'No, McNeil was the major player.'

'And yet he sits relatively undisturbed in a care home. Interesting.'

'What?' asked Hope on seeing the woman's furrowed brow.

'It's not really about the event, is it? It's about revenge, but it's about telling the world by going for something big. They'll go for something, but why two? Why two methods of destruction?' said Anna. 'Two weapons that make little sense together? Short-range and a long-range attack. Something's not right. Something doesn't sit here.'

Suddenly, the woman stopped and turned back to Hope.

'I told you what happened, Detective Inspector. Any more questions, call me on the appropriate number.'

'What are you off to do now?'

'Dig,' said Anna Hunt. 'Dig and look deeper into the background of Isla Bishop. Try to work out what's going on. Something doesn't smell right; something doesn't sit right. Take care of Macleod. I think he could be in trouble.'

'Like he's not in trouble already?' said Hope.

'I don't think he really is yet.' Anna walked off without looking back and Ross approached Hope.

'Do you have any good information?'

'No, not really,' said Hope, 'but she's worried, and that bothers me.'

Scene break. Scene break. Scene break.

Clarissa had been digging for most of the night and now was sitting back rather smugly at her desk. She had images of the woman who committed suicide in Aviemore, the woman who had lived at the flat she had gone to earlier. The report of the incident was sitting on her desk, and she pored through it, reading with intent. Several times she stopped and re-read.

The woman had been found hanging in her own room. Beneath her had been a child, a thirteen-year-old girl. A seventeen-year-old boy had come back into the room, and it was he who had phoned the police. The girl had just sat there while the woman hanged.

The woman's name wasn't Mary Smith. It was Agnes Greenhalgh which sent Clarissa off on another chase into the records, looking for when Agnes Greenhalgh had turned up in the world. She had only surfaced around the time of Macleod joining the police force. This made Clarissa wonder, but she needed confirmation. Was this the woman and, if so, where were her children?

As she sat looking at the report in front of her, Clarissa glanced over. Patterson was working his own way through the computer system. He'd been tasked with tracing Mary Smith. The records were old, and it was hard to find where she was, but the man was diligent. Clarissa stared at him. She was finding it difficult to have him around her in the office. Every time she looked, he wasn't the smartly dressed, reasonably confident young man that sat there now. Instead, she saw a neck covered in blood.

She looked down at her own hands and for a moment Clarissa saw the red that was on them that night. Her mind became full again of screaming. Screaming for an ambulance, holding his neck, keeping the man alive. She remembered stepping back when the paramedics had arrived, looking at her hands.

That was the thing about it. The little green car had been fixed. Seoras had tidied it up, put it back together new. Patterson was physically standing here new. He looked well. He looked good, but no one put the trauma away as easily as that.

Clarissa was a mess inside. She knew why she was here. She was here for Seoras because things weren't over yet. Seoras was in danger, and she'd always come to help him. She was, after all, a detective, and this was one of her colleagues. A colleague, that yes, she liked a lot but she'd do it for any of them.

'Have you had any trauma?'

'What?' asked Patterson.

'Have you had any trauma, Patterson, from that night?'

'I got my throat slashed.' he said. 'They had to stitch it up. I had to heal up. I had tubes inserted down me for however long. Lost a stack of blood. Is that not enough trauma?'

'No, I don't mean the physical trauma, I mean mental.'

'What like?' he asked.

'Well, like anything.'

'Yes,' he said. 'Counsellor said it might go away with time, but it might not. Why do you ask?'

'Because mine isn't going away. Every time I look at you, I see you with a slashed throat. My hands are on you. I see the blood on my hands.'

'Sorry,' he said. 'I get flashbacks too, but slightly different. I don't remember a lot after the knife cut, but I thank you,' he said. 'I really do. You saved my...'

'Don't go there. We'd all do it for each other. That's what we do.'

'But you're still suffering,' said Patterson. 'Can I help?'

'In what way?' asked Clarissa. 'In what way can you help? I'm getting counselling. There's a man in my life who's helping me. I've...'

'You're worried this could happen again, aren't you?'

She nodded. Patterson was insightful. What was her greatest fear, that she'd have to do this again? That this wasn't a one-off? She'd already had to charge into Macleod's rescue. She had to put this killer down. He had to be stopped. She had to finish this one off. It suddenly occurred to her it wasn't about Macleod anymore, it was about her. It had truly got personal.

'As I said, anything I can do, let me know.'

'Have you got anywhere with the work you're doing, though?' asked Clarissa.

'Come here a minute, sergeant,' he said.

Clarissa gave a nod and stood behind Patterson. He pointed at the screen. 'Mary Smith spent some time in Aviemore and she had repeated sessions for the abuse she had. At that time, it wasn't normal that you got counselling. Counselling really wasn't as strong as it is today, so the fact she was going through that shows how bad it was for her. I think it must have driven her to suicide.'

'I think you might be right,' said Clarissa. 'When you read the report, her daughter was with her, sitting there watching her. It's only when the older brother got back that he called the police.'

'So what? The girl just sat there?'

'They don't think she came in with her. They think she sat

and watched Agnes while she hanged.'

'Dear God,' said Patterson, 'that's bleak. She must have…'

'It must have been so bad for her mother that the girl would choose to sit there and almost be happier for her to do that than to save her.'

'Well, before the suicide, Mary Smith is in Aviemore for a couple of years getting this therapy, and then after that, she just disappears off the grid.'

Clarissa looked at the earliest mention of Greenhalgh in the flat. She looked at when the name of Mary Smith stopped appearing on records.

'The timing of the switch is perfect,' she said. 'I know it's all circumstantial. There's no proof, but it looks like Mary Smith hung herself because of the abuse she had suffered, and it looks like her daughter watched.

'So, we got a possible trace,' said Clarissa. 'Mary Smith becomes Greenhalgh. Greenhalgh dies in the flat, suicide. Then we have the robber Greenhalgh, whose last address is there, who's now off the grid and whose hair was grabbed by Macleod at the home. I think we know who's coming after Seoras,' said Clarissa to the air. 'But how do we find them?'

Chapter 22

Ross had returned to the station and was sitting in the office staring at the note that had been left to Macleod. It was a strange tale, and at first glance, made little sense. The office was busy, Hope running here and there amongst everyone trying to track down Greenhalgh, wherever he could be. Susan and Clarissa had disappeared out of the office, off to see Macleod, but with the fervour that was going on, Ross was finding it difficult to concentrate.

He never had this in the past, and he wondered what was happening to him. Ross was a man of the office. He could sit there and send people left, right, and centre. He could deal with many things coming in and out, but at the moment, he was struggling to focus. Every phone being put down, every turn and step, even a request for coffee, was taking his mind away from the piece of paper he was looking at.

He picked it up, along with a pen, strolled out of the office and down to the station canteen. He grabbed a cup of coffee and then sat at the table in the far corner. There were a few people around at this hour, and he gave a sigh of relief.

What was wrong with him? What was going on? He knew he'd faced trauma recently, but it had been all right, hadn't it?

It was all getting back to normal. It was…

He looked down at his hand, shaking. Why was he shaking? What was the big deal here? He looked at the note in front of him, and suddenly Ross felt an overwhelming sense of panic. This was on him, wasn't it? He was the code breaker. He was the guy who could get into ciphers and riddles. They had a large rocket launching device. They had a suicide vest. He needed to come up with where this was. He needed to break this.

His mind went back to Angus being shot, and then he stopped thinking and puffed. He could feel the sweat on his brow. That's what it was. Methodical as ever, Ross had worked it out. His problem was if he didn't solve this, something was going to happen in the same way that it happened to Angus.

He'd always been so detached, always been capable of ignoring the effects of what had happened to other people. Not now. It hadn't just happened to him, but to Angus. It had happened to the man he was sharing his life with, and it had been so close to happening to Daniel, their little adopted boy. Ross wiped his brow and looked down at the paper.

The ticking down of the nuclear clock. What on earth did that mean? Back-to-back beaches separated by a clock. No idea. The destruction of the house of Bute. It made no sense. It made absolutely no sense. What was the character in this meant to do? How would he destroy the house of Bute? Where on earth was the house of Bute? Ross thought he knew his Scottish history well, but Bute? It wasn't ringing a bell with him. Back to back beaches, the town by the sea. Half of Scotland was beside the sea. The sea played such a big part in all of Scottish life. That wasn't a clue.

He looked down at his hand again; it was shaking. 'Focus,

Ross,' he said. 'Focus, calm down and focus.'

There was a noise. It was Patterson coming down to the canteen to get something to eat. Ross stood up.

'Peace and bloody quiet,' he said to himself. 'Peace and bloody quiet is what I need. I need to be nowhere near noise.'

He strode out, leaving an astonished Patterson in his wake, and went to the bottom of the building where the records guys lived. Ross stepped inside and plonked himself down at a desk, much to the stares of the records team. He gave no explanation as to why he was there. He put the bit of paper down on a table.

Ross stared at it, breaking down each word, trying to come to some conclusion about what he was seeing. There were voices. People were whispering, talking. He looked up. There was a man. He thought he was called Johnson. He was talking. There was tapping on the typewriter, the hum of the machine.

Ross stood up, grabbed the piece of paper, turned, and with an almighty shout, said, 'Bloody hell, can I get no damn peace,' and marched clean out of the room.

Behind him, the hum of the computers continued, but the tapping on the keyboard stopped. Everyone looked at the swinging door in surprise for at least ten seconds, then they looked at each other, raised shoulders and returned to their work.

Scene break, scene break, scene break.

'Here,' said Hope, handing a cup of coffee to Anna Hunt. Anna had come into the station and was now giving one of her characteristic wry smiles towards Hope.

'Your team's done good work,' said Anna. 'From what I read,

I think it's clear that Mary Smith's son has got something to do with this. She changed her name to Greenhalgh. He's now involved, and he's quite the character, and he's astute. Likes to come at things from a different angle. He took out the ministers, first of all, to build himself up a group, but I'm thinking that the whole time, this is where it's been going. Problem we've got is,' said Anna, 'we have got nothing on him, he's a nobody. He literally is a nobody. No social security number, no taxes paid, no wages going in. Where is he getting all this from? How is he shoring up the group?'

'Is that not why he's done the group,' said Hope, 'to get money fed in? Can't have been easy to generate the money. I know some people we've brought in were reasonably wealthy. There's talk of spouses not realising that money had been taken from accounts.'

'So what we're reckoning,' said Anna, 'is that he's turned around and started off these original two ideas to bring in finances?'

'I think so,' said Hope. 'I think this has been his goal all along, what he's about to do.'

'Do we know what he's about to do?' asked Anna. 'Other than attack an...'

'He's going to attack somebody very, very important,' said Hope, 'and we've got to get there first.'

'Are you sure that's the plan? You're sure that's what it is?'

'It's the way I see it.'

'What about his sister?' asked Anna.

'Nothing on her. The kids were separated according to the report of the suicide, but we can't find anything on her. It seems that she disappeared. She certainly doesn't seem to be wandering around within the name Greenhalgh anymore.

We've traced through. We can't find any woman with the name Greenhalgh.'

'If she was adopted, though.'

'She was,' said Hope. 'I've traced that through as well. It appears that she disappeared from a foster home when she was sixteen. Not been seen since.'

Anna Hunt's face tightened, and Hope could see that the woman was worried.

'You think she's important in this?'

'Possibly,' said Anna, 'but you can't find her. I'm going to see if I can. I'll be around, though. We're coming close to what's going to happen. He wouldn't have left that note with Seoras, that description, that whatever it is, unless it was coming to an endgame.'

Anna gulped her coffee, stood up, and left the office, leaving Hope sitting in her chair. She could feel her left hand beginning to shake again. It didn't help that Anna was pointing out they were coming to a climax. It didn't help that the pressure was piling on. 'Process,' she told herself. 'Keep going through your process.' Maybe Clarissa would come up with something now that she was over to see Macleod. Maybe. Just maybe.

Scene break, scene break, scene break.

'How are you doing, Seoras?' asked Clarissa.

He was sitting outside on a bench looking out towards the beach. Susan Cunningham was sitting about ten feet away, looking at her phone.

'Where's Jane?' he asked. 'Is she safe?'

'She's with Frank,' said Clarissa, 'and I've got plenty of people around him. I don't think Jane is the target, though.'

Macleod looked off into the distance and then turned back and nodded. 'I agree,' he said, 'but I don't want to take the risk in case I'm wrong.'

'You didn't take a risk. You left her with me,' said Clarissa. 'She'll be fine. Ross is working away on your message. It's a bit of a strange one.

'I've got something for you,' said Clarissa. 'I know you've told us all along you didn't know Mary Smith. You only knew Mairi. Well, here's Mary Smith.'

She showed Macleod the face of a woman who was deceased.'

'Where is that from?' he asked.

'It's from the report from the suicide. You recognise her at all?'

'No,' said Macleod. 'Not at all. I mean, she could have been on the island, but there's a good number of people on the island. I was young. You don't know everyone.'

'So I'm assuming she wasn't in any of the church congregations, or anything like you were in?'

'She certainly didn't make herself known in public, particularly,' said Macleod. 'It's definitely not Mairi Smith. Mary had a much thinner chin, more developed cheekbones.'

'Okay,' said Clarissa. 'I think I might take it over to McNeil. I want to know more about the woman's son. That's the key thing. Maybe he'll know. Maybe he was still holding back on me.'

'He held back on me,' said Macleod.

'Yeah, but you're easy to hold back on,' said Clarissa, and drew a frown from Macleod. 'No, seriously. He knows that you'll just keep asking him questions. I might physically hit him.'

Macleod gave her a small chortle, but then he looked back at

Clarissa. 'You put whatever pressure you need to on him. We need to get this guy. Whatever it is he's going to do, it will not be good, and I have a feeling when he does, it may involve me.'

'Cunningham's here though,' she said.

'And there's a couple of other plain-clothed policemen about. Susan hasn't told me who they are, but I can tell who they are. She didn't want to say, but it's pretty obvious.' Macleod raised his voice for the last couple of sentences, and Clarissa looked over at Cunningham, who was deliberately ignoring the man.

'It's for the best. You're not at your finest at the moment.'

'Is this what we're down to?' asked Macleod. 'Pushing McNeil?'

'We can't find them. They drop out of the system. Maybe McNeil would know where they went. Maybe there's other family on the mainland. He'll know. Got to push everything at the moment.'

'Yes, you do,' said Macleod. 'You do.' Clarissa walked away to the front of the care home and called in to Hope.

'How is he?'

'Oh, he's as well as it'd be expected. He's frustrated. He wants to be solving this himself.'

'I can imagine. What's the protection like?'

'Cunningham sorted them out fine. She's vetting everybody that comes in, and she's hanging around close to him.'

'I want to talk to McNeil again, show him my face. See if he knows more. I don't trust him, Hope, and we haven't got a lot else to go on.'

'It's kind of putting you guys out there, isn't it? Taking you away from where you could be useful here.'

'It's a hunch,' said Clarissa, 'and besides, if we're actually finding out what's going on, you'd be calling Anna Hunt. We'll not be taking this down, will we? She'll not want anything risked. That's why she's staying close to you. She doesn't know what's going to happen. She doesn't know where it's going to happen. Trust me. You tell her what you think is going to happen and she will flood the area with people, and a good thing too, we shouldn't be taking out people like this. That should be their job. They don't have to operate within certain boundaries.'

'Okay,' said Hope. 'You can go over but given the threat level and given what's going on, take Cunningham with you.'

'But what about Macleod?'

'You said Cunningham's got the protection there. Step it up. I think there may be more people there than you realise as well.'

'Anna Hunt?'

'Yes. She thinks it might be aimed at Seoras as well.

'If that's the case, wouldn't you keep somebody close to him?'

'Okay,' said Clarissa. 'I'll tell Cunningham she's coming with me. We'll get over to Lewis as quick as we can, then go down and see McNeil.'

'You think you can get there by tonight?'

'Yes, we'll get the ferry across. We should get in there by about nine o'clock. We'll get down and see him first thing in the morning.'

'Good idea,' said Hope. 'Stay safe, Clarissa.'

'You too.' Clarissa hung up the call. Hope was telling her to stay safe. She really was worried.

Chapter 23

Ross was having a terrible day. He'd wandered around trying to find somewhere quiet, but nothing was quiet. Everything was annoying him. Everything. He was struggling to believe he could be so affected by a case, so affected by nothing. Why was he hearing all this noise all the time? Why was there no space, no room, to just be himself, a bunker to just exist and work in? Was everything becoming a bother to him?

He was now sitting in the office with Patterson across from him. At least Patterson was quiet. Ross had cut up the message left for Macleod, little pieces across his desk. Not individual words, but strings of words to work out even where to begin. His take was that it was apocryphal writing. They were images to portray something else. What was the code?

He had tried looking at ciphers. Had it been the letters? No. Had it been patterns of words within it? No. Maybe it was just plain apocryphal writing. Maybe it was just images of places. Could he fix a place in any of the descriptions?

He looked at the small piece in front of him. *Destruction of the House of Bute.* He leaned back and stretched. *What on earth? Who in Scotland was in the Bute family? Was in the Bute clan.* He looked over at Patterson, who was staring back at him.

'Do you not go home?' asked Patterson.

'We need to crack this,' he said. 'We need to crack this badly.'

'Well, maybe I could have a stab at it,' he said.

'Have you worked with ciphers or codes or things like that before?' asked Ross.

'No,' said Patterson, 'but I'm game.'

Ross threw one at him, even if it was just to keep the man quiet so we could work.

'It's talking about the destruction of the House of Bute. Where's that clan?'

Patterson looked stumped. 'I don't know about the clan,' he said. 'The First Minister lives in the House of Bute.'

Ross stared at him. How could he miss it? How did he miss that? He grabbed the small bit of paper saying the destruction of the House of Bute and tore from his desk straight over to Hope's office. He opened the door without even knocking. She was sitting with her feet up on the desk, reading a report.

'Destruction of the House of Bute.'

'Yes,' said Hope.

'That's the First Minister's address. He lives in the House of Bute.'

'They're going after the first minister?' Hope stood up quickly, grabbed the phone in front of her, and punched in a recently learned number.

'This is Anna Hunt. How can I help you, Detective Inspector?'

'Ross has just bust the code, well, part of it. It talks about the destruction of the House of Bute. That's where the First Minister lives.'

'It is,' said Anna Hunt, 'but the First Minister's not there.'

183

'It's what it says. I suggest you increase the security.'

'I don't think you're right on this,' said Anna. 'The First Minister's not there. If he's not there, it's just a house. Why blow it up? These guys aren't terrorists in the sense that they just destroy places. They kill people. All this time he's killed people, he has never just destroyed a place, but I'll check it out.'

Hope put the phone down as the call was closed from Anna Hunt's end.

'She's not convinced, Ross,' said Hope. 'Yes, it is the First Minister's residence, but the First Minister's not there. He's in a safe place because they're visiting elsewhere.'

'Visiting elsewhere?' queried Ross. He turned without acknowledging Hope any further and walked back to his desk. He looked down at the pieces of paper in front of him, the ticking down of the nuclear clock. What on earth was the nuclear clock and ticking down? He sat back, thinking about it literally. What would it mean? What could you call something?

Of course, he thought, *the nuclear clock. That was the way they measured how close you were to oblivion.' It was a Cold War thing, wasn't it? Even more than that, they used to say that you would tell how close we were to nuclear war by where that clock got to. And the worst case it had got to was...*

He stopped, a sudden chill running through him. *Two minutes to midnight.* He looked down at the other pieces of paper. *The town by the sea and the back-to-back beaches that are separated by the clock. Back-to-back beaches, separated by a clock?* Ross sat back. *Where could that be? That's not a standard landmark*, he thought. *That's very specific, but it's not a...*

'It was worth a punt,' he decided. Maybe Macleod would know. If a lot of this was about Macleod, then just maybe... Ross picked up the phone and got a rather annoyed care worker

184

on the front desk of the care home ask him did he know what time it was.

'I don't care,' he said. 'Wake up Seoras Macleod and tell him DC Ross is on the call. I need him now.'

It took a couple of minutes before Macleod came wearily onto the phone.

'I'm working on your note that was left. I need to know, sir, are there beaches in Stornoway?'

'There are beaches all round the Isle of Lewis.'

'No,' said Ross, 'specifically Stornoway.'

'Well, "beach" is probably an overused term for it. They have two sides in Stornoway. There's what's called North Beach and there's South Beach, but South Beach is actually a harbour. North Beach, you barely see the beach unless it's… well, low tide. There's a representation of the "Iolaire" there. That's a boat that sunk up here, back at the end of World War I. They've marked it out in the sand with these pillars. One for each person who died, but it wasn't there back in my day. It's more recent.'

'But they're known as North and South Beach,' said Ross.

'Yes,' said Macleod. 'North and South Beach car parks. That's what everybody calls them.'

'Is there a clock between them?'

'What?' asked Macleod. 'What do you mean?'

'Is there a clock between them? Is there somewhere where there is a clock between them?'

'Town Hall,' said Macleod. 'There's a clock up in the town hall. The town hall sits between North and South Beach.'

Ross could feel a chill. He looked at the time. It said eleven forty-five PM.

He raced to Hope's office, leaving Macleod hanging on the

185

call. He burst through the door and shouted, 'Have we got anyone in Stornoway?'

'Clarissa's there, stopping the night. She went down to see McNeil. He didn't have—'

'Shut up,' said Ross, suddenly, and Hope's face went angry.

'What the hell do you mean, shut—-'

'Shut up,' said Ross. 'We need to get on the phone. It's happening.'

'What's happening?'

'First Minister lives in Bute House. It's a destruction of the house of Bute. Nuclear clock. Two minutes to midnight. It's eleven forty-five. We haven't got long. They must get out.'

'I don't get what you mean, Ross.'

Ross picked up his mobile and called Clarissa's number.

'Check for me,' said Ross, as the call was ringing. 'Check for me. That list of people, very important people, where they are, where they're going to be. Today and tomorrow, is anyone in Stornoway?'

Hope pulled up a computer screen and started looking while Ross was on the phone to Clarissa.

'It's blooming the middle of the night,' said Clarissa. 'What are you calling for? I told Hope we've got nothing for McNeil, nothing.'

'It's not McNeil I need to know about. You need to get out onto the street between North Beach and South Beach, somewhere out there. First Minister's coming, and going to be attacked.'

'What?' bellowed Clarissa.

'He's attacking the First Minister.'

'Ross,' said Hope suddenly. 'He's arriving on a boat tonight coming into Stornoway Harbour. Special commemorative boat. That's why he's travelling on it. It's got a mast.'

'Clarissa, there's a boat coming in. It's got a mast. It's an old-style boat. I think he's going to blow it up. I think he's intending to kill the First Minister.'

Ross heard the shout for Cunningham yelled by Clarissa.

'Tell Anna Hunt,' said Ross to Hope. 'See if she's got anyone there. See if they can get hold of the master on the boat. Maybe they can turn the boat around.'

Hope grabbed the phone. Her hands were shaking as she dialled the number.

Scene break, scene break, scene break.

Clarissa was running towards Stornoway's seafront with Susan Cunningham behind her. It was more of a hobble and less of a run from Clarissa. She could see the large mast of a vessel on the outreaches of Stornoway Harbour.

'That's the boat,' said Clarissa. 'That's the boat. He's got to be about here somewhere, Cunningham. Can you see someone?'

They scanned, looking here and there, but could see no one.

'If it's coming in, it's going to sail towards the piers. Maybe he'll be here. You check the far pier, I'll check this one. See if we can find him.'

Clarissa watched Susan Cunningham sprint off, her hair tied up behind her. She reminded Clarissa so much of Hope. Meanwhile, with her shawl hastily thrown round her and in her tartan trews, Clarissa clomped her way over to the nearer pier. As she walked up to the gates, which were locked, she stared through, trying to see if the man was there. Her phone then rang.

'He's on this pier,' said Cunningham. 'I can see him. He's got

187

the rocket launcher on his shoulder.'

'Go,' said Clarissa, 'I'm on my way.' She put her phone away, turned and began hobbling towards the other pier. She was far behind. Along the street beside her came a motorbike and Clarissa stepped out in front of it. She held up her warrant card.

'Get off the bike. I require it. I need to use your bike.'

'No, you don't,' said the man on it. He was dressed in full biker gear.

'I said off. This is police business. I need your bike now.'

'What gives you the right to…'

Clarissa didn't have time for this. She reached forward, grabbed the man by the collar, and pulled hard. He put two hands on her arm, trying to force her away from him, but she'd learnt a trick or two in her time. With her other hand, she grabbed one of his, took the thumb and bent it backwards. The man screamed. His arms shot off her, and that gave her the chance to put a second hand on him.

She pulled hard. The bike tipped over and the man fell to the ground. She reached down, grabbed the bike, and pulled it up. The man was shouting at her, 'You can't do this,' but she didn't care. With the bike now upright again, she clambered on, started it again, and raced off to the far pier.

As Clarissa approached the pier, she realised the gates were slightly open. The man must have been out where the public wasn't meant to go. As she drove through the gate, she could see Cunningham, up ahead.

Susan called to the man, and he turned to Cunningham, the missile launcher still on his shoulder. He set it down and as she arrived. He stepped to one side, grabbed her, and literally threw her down on the ground. Without hesitation, he took a large kick at her head. Clarissa winced as she saw Cunningham's neck whip sideways.

The man heard the motorbike, and he bent down. Picking up the missile launcher again, he turned to face the wooden ship that was now sailing into the harbour. He wasn't far away from it. He couldn't miss.

Clarissa raced towards him. She had two options. She could stop the bike, tell him to stop, but the missile would be fired by then. Anyway, he would not stop. He was a lunatic.

Clarissa opened up the throttle as much as she dared, racing towards the end of the pier. She suddenly realised she wouldn't stop. She couldn't control the bike, get off and take him down. Susan had been practically dismissed by him.

Clarissa was getting closer, and she tried to slide the bike. She pulled on the front brake, the back of the bike whipped round, and from ten feet away, the bike slid towards him. Clarissa screamed as she fell backwards off the bike. Ahead of her, it caught the large man by the legs, knocking him off into the sea. The missile fired somewhere up into the sky. The man had disappeared into the gloom beyond the end of the pier, and Clarissa sailed off after him.

She hit the water. A cold enveloped her instantly.

Don't panic, said something inside her. *Don't panic, cold water, relax, relax...* but inside, she was gasping. Inside, she was panicking. She tried to flail with her legs, kick out, but she didn't feel like she was moving anywhere. She was still in the water. Her shawl was heavy around her, but she'd done it, she thought. She'd taken him out. He was down here in the water. He wouldn't be coming back up. She'd hit him with a bike. How could he? His legs would be mangled. He would be incapable of surviving, surely. She opened her eyes, but the

189

water was too dark. She had got him, though.

It was like a deep peace enveloping her. There was suddenly no panic. Even if she didn't surface, Seoras would be all right. He'd be fine. It'd be calm again. Frank would miss her, and she'd miss Frank, but she'd done what she set out to do. She'd stopped this man from killing Macleod. There was peace in knowing that as she sank.

A hand grabbed her wrist. Suddenly, someone had an arm underneath her arm and was pushing her up towards the surface. Clarissa broke through, and the cold air surrounded her. She gasped desperately.

'Got you,' said Susan Cunningham. 'Got you.'

Clarissa felt herself being dragged over to the stanchion by the edge of the pier. There was a bit of metal sticking out from it, and Susan Cunningham was holding onto that. Her other arm was holding onto Clarissa. She was shouting, 'Help,' screaming for help, but Clarissa was completely calm. *Going to be all right, Seoras*, she said to herself. *You're going to be all right. I got him.*

Chapter 24

'But she's going to be fine?' asked Hope.

'Yes, they're just keeping her in for observation. Clarissa's also sore here and there. She's got some flesh wounds running up her leg and backside where she slid off the bike, but no bones are broken. She's okay.'

'You did well, both of you.'

'It's a bit embarrassing though,' said Susan Cunningham, 'getting taken out by him. If it hadn't had been for Clarissa, that boat would've been on fire. We'd have lost our First Minister.'

'But we didn't,' said Hope. 'That's what you have to focus on. We didn't. You learn the lessons before the next time, but we didn't lose our First Minister.'

'Are you having a bit of a party in there?' asked Susan, hearing the commotion in the background of the telephone call.

'Well, we've still got a lot of cleanup to do and that, but you got him. So, we celebrate.'

'Well, we didn't get him. He's disappeared down to the bottom. Maybe he'll show up in a few days,' said Susan.

'But Seoras is safe, Jane's safe, they're all safe, and these crazy killings have stopped. You were a big part of that, Cunningham.

Susan, you deserve a lot of credit. You and Clarissa as well. Thank goodness for Ross.'

'He must be relieved,' said Susan. 'He took Angus being shot so badly.'

'Keep an eye on him. I'm not sure he's got over that at all.'

Hope put down the phone, and sat back in her chair. In front of her was a glass of sparkling wine. It was rare any bottles were opened inside the station, but in this case, she thought there was more than a good reason to celebrate. Still, she was the boss now, so she wasn't going mad with it; just the one glass.

Outside in the outer office, the atmosphere was much more celebratory. She saw some of them occasionally hugging each other and Ross looking a lot happier than he'd been in the last couple of months. Her team was intact, albeit just about, and she sunk back into her chair, allowing it to support her. It had been rough the last while, really rough, but they'd come out of it.

It was then she noticed someone coming into the outer office. There was a black pair of trousers and a jacket, black again. It was a woman given the figure, but there was no clip across the office floor, and then the door to her office opened.

Normally, people would knock. Any of the team would knock unless they were in panic mode or desperately wanted to feel Hope's wrath. The woman who entered, Hope suspected, knocked for very few people. She closed the door behind her and walked quietly over to Hope's desk.

'Your people did well.'

'Thank you, Miss Hunt,' said Hope. 'Pleasure to work with you. They did do well. They nearly didn't come back from it.'

'No, and in fairness, quite an idea to hit him with the bike.

She's very tenacious, his Rottweiler, isn't she?'

'Very much so,' said Hope. 'I guess she's probably a little past it, age-wise, to do your sort of work.'

'She's not subtle enough for my sort of work,' said Anna, 'but she has her place and she does what she does very well. I can understand why Macleod has her. I've been told they haven't found the body.'

'His body's still down there somewhere. We don't believe he got out. If she hit him with the motorbike, his legs probably would've broken. I would suspect he didn't last long at all. A pity,' said Hope. 'I would have liked to see him stand justice.'

'Really?' queried Anna. 'You'd have wanted that face looking back at the people he had hurt. People like that are beyond simple murderer. People like that, it's better if it's just ended. I can see a sort of justice in it.'

'I guess that's that," said Hope. 'It's been a pleasure working with you.' She extended her hand, but Anna didn't even flinch.

'What makes you think that's that?'

'I just said if his leg's broken, he'll probably be dead.'

'We recovered the missile that was in the harbour,' said Anna. 'We haven't recovered his body, but there was also a suicide vest that went missing.'

'So what are you saying?' asked Hope. 'He's given that to someone else?'

'I don't know,' said Anna, 'but I'm thinking this isn't over yet.'

She turned and walked out of the room, leaving Hope at her desk. Before she could think any further, her phone rang. Picking it up, she heard a cheerful voice on the other end.

'Am I still doing the paperwork?' asked Jim, the Assistant Chief Constable.

'Bloody right, you are,' said Hope. 'I've got to patch up my wounded Rottweiller.'

'She is quite something,' said Jim. 'Really something. I can't believe she came back. I was worried after the Patterson thing.'

'She was back for a reason,' said Hope. 'With that reason gone, we'll wait and see how she is.'

'You think that'll be her?'

'I don't know,' said Hope. 'I wish not, but she did just get married.'

'Well,' said Jim, 'either way, well done. Have you spoken to Macleod yet?'

'No, I was letting Seoras get his beauty sleep. In saying that, he should be up soon. I'll call him.'

Hope put down the phone, happy that at least Jim appreciated the job done. It could only help her standing. This was her first real time in charge. She had no cover. Yes, Jim was there, but not really. She was acting DCI or part of it at least. There was plenty to be happy about. She called Macleod, and after waiting to be put through to him, she heard a groggy voice on the other end.

'Did you sleep well?' Hope asked.

'It doesn't work like that,' said Macleod. 'I saw him in my dreams last night. I woke up about three or four times.'

'But he's dead, Seoras. You know that. Clarissa slid into him with a motorbike. She took him to the bottom of Stornoway Harbour, and Cunningham pulled only her back out. Clarissa's lucky to be alive, but she stopped our First Minister from being blown to smithereens. She's quite the hero.'

'She's okay then?' asked Macleod.

'Susan says she'll be in the hospital for a day or two, just observation. I've managed to get Frank on the way over to her.'

'Where's Jane?'

'Jane's got plenty of people still around her at the moment, but anyway, not that it matters anymore.'

'The guards have been pulled from here,' he said. 'The two plainclothes people, they're gone.'

'I did check,' said Hope. 'We didn't put plainclothes people there.'

'No, you didn't,' said Macleod. 'They weren't that sort of plainclothes. You were working with Anna Hunt, weren't you?'

'Yes,' said Hope. 'You think Anna put them there?'

'They're gone though,' said Macleod. 'She must think the danger's over.'

'You don't?'

'He had a sister. He had a sister we can't trace,' said Macleod. 'who may have another weapon, a suicide jacket. Greenhalgh never would've taken a suicide jacket. It's not what he was about. Remember, that girl watched her mother die. That girl let her mother die, commit suicide in front of her face because she thought that was the better way out. That anger has to go somewhere,' said Macleod.

'I think Jane's going to come down and see you soon.'

There was silence on the other end of the phone, and then it was put down. *He really was hurt*, thought Hope. *He really is battered*. She hoped counselling could help him, but she couldn't help at this point in time. She'd done what she could.

Hope picked up her glass off the desk, stood up, and walked to the office door. She had to be there for the celebration. You had to be the one happy and smiling because you caught him, even though you felt exhausted. Hope put on a radiant face and stepped through her office door.

Scene break, scene break, scene break.

Macleod was all over the place. The man stalking him had died. Ross had managed to solve whatever puzzle had been thrown at him. Clarissa had taken the killer out. His team had come to the rescue, Hope overseeing it all. The new people pitching in as best they could, should have been happy. The team functioning without him. At the end of the day, that was the point, wasn't it? That's why you built a team. That's why you were a leader, to disappear eventually. Hope had come through. They had got their man, but he wasn't happy.

One thing he was aware of was that Hope didn't think like him. There was still a suicide vest out there. Hope would think that was Anna Hunt's problem and, in a lot of ways, it was. Military tech had gone missing, it needed to be recovered, so who better than military special services? Who better than the secret people behind the country? Macleod's people did not know about arms dealers. It was outwith their remit, outwith what they did. Anna Hunt did. Anna Hunt knew all about them. She had taken away the protection, so surely it must be okay now.

Something was bothering him. He walked to the far end of the care home. There was a small headland. He thought about walking down, heading to the beach, but as he walked along the grass, he saw someone coming up from the beach, creeping towards him.

It was a woman. She had some sort of large coat on. As she got closer, he felt on edge. He studied her features. He recognised the woman from the photograph, Mary Smith. This was Mary Smith? She looked so like her. It must be her, but Mary Smith was dead. Mary Smith had hanged herself.

Macleod felt like screaming at his own mind. Why was he being shown this now? Surely everything was at rest, wasn't it? The figure kept coming towards him.

'You killed her,' said a voice. 'Macleod, you let this happen to her and you killed her. You sent her away. I watched,' she said, 'I watched her hang herself. I sat there. It was her only way out. Nothing. Nothing could stop what was happening, all the terrors coming back to her. That's why it's coming back to you.'

'I didn't know a Mary Smith,' said Macleod. 'I didn't know any Mary Smith. I knew Mairi, but you're not Mary Smith either, are you?'

'You killed her. McNeil and you killed her. You killed my brother, too.'

Macleod watched the woman take off her jacket. Around her in a vest were small explosives. Small but no doubt deadly to those within range.

'It's time to pay your debts, Macleod. It's time to pay your debts. Vengeance is mine, it's not God's, it's not anybody else's. It's mine because I saw what you did. I saw what happened to her. I saw what not recognising the pain and the hurt did. I recognised what that did to her. She was sent away like some little slut, but he abused her. He was the one and my mother left me. My mother left me when I was still so young.'

'Enough,' said Macleod. 'It wasn't me. It wasn't me.'

'Your name was there.'

'It's before me. It's another Macleod.'

'No, it's you. You are the police, anyway. I don't care if you were there or not. This will tell them. This will teach them. You're a man from the island. She said you were all the same.'

Macleod dropped to his knees, watching as the woman

reached down for a switch, taking it out in her hand.

'Don't do this,' said Macleod. 'Don't do this. There's no need. It's all done.'

'There's every need. It still happens. Things still occur. Women are still left like this. You'll burn for it.'

'But you'll burn too,' said Macleod. 'You're innocent. You don't…'

'Innocent? None of us are innocent. Especially not you. Vengeance is mine. You hear me, Macleod? Mine.'

On his knees, Seoras Macleod watched as the woman raised her thumb, ready to press down on the trigger that would activate the vest. He was so close to her. It would be over. Dear God, it would be over. He prayed for intervention. He prayed for help. His heart beat furiously and his stomach went sick.

The bang was loud. His ears were deafened, and the second one that followed in incredibly quick succession caused a ringing sensation throughout his head. He watched as Miss Greenhalgh, in her vest, lifted off the ground and landed after the second shot. It was like watching slow-motion, and he could not turn his head away before she hit the ground. Before he could react and stand up, someone ran over incredibly quickly and stood over the woman. A gun was pointing at the head of Miss Greenhalgh.

'Are you okay, Detective Chief Inspector?'

He looked up, and for a moment, he thought he saw Kirsten Stewart. The black trousers, the black top, a small but powerful figure with black hair running down the back, but then he saw the face was older and had a wry smile on it.

'This is it,' said Anna Hunt. 'It's done, Macleod, over! You need to start getting better.'

Chapter 25

It was a month after the demise of the Greenhalghs. Macleod was finally getting home. He had returned to his house along with Jane, but things just didn't feel the same. There were still episodes. He was still having a problem. He was more in control now, though.

Now that he knew that there wasn't somebody there, he climbed up the steps and, instead of heading for his office, he walked over to the main office. From there, he entered through to Hope's private office. She stood almost at attention, smiling as he came in.

'You can stop that,' he said. Her hair was down, cascading onto her shoulders. She wore jeans and a T-shirt on top. She looked radiant, truly radiant.

'Congratulations,' said Macleod. 'Your first one on your own, first one truly all on your own.'

'Learnt from the best,' she said.

'Now, this wasn't about me, this was about you. This was horrible. You had to keep going. You had to keep going despite what I was going through. This is all yours,' he said.

'Hardly,' said Hope. 'Ross solved the clue. Clarissa and Susan stopped the man while he was preparing to blow up our First

Minister. Patterson stood up and contributed while injured.'

'That's your team,' said Macleod. 'That's your team, and you had to trust them. You even liaised in with Anna Hunt.'

'But I didn't see it, did I?' she said. 'I didn't see the Greenhalgh woman.'

'That's why you need somebody like me on your team. You're going to need someone.'

'I don't,' she said.

'When I'm gone, you're going to need someone. You're going to have to find them. Kirsten would have been good. Kirsten's got my sort of mind. I take it Anna didn't say she was hoping to make a return.'

'No, she didn't,' said Hope. Macleod looked up and saw tears in Hope's eyes.

'I'm not gone,' he said. 'I said when I'm gone. The old man's not gone yet.'

'Do you know what the hardest part was? Do you know what it was, Seoras? It was watching you suffer. At first when they kidnapped you, and then when he tormented you in that home and now, now you're looking over my shoulder, aren't you?'

'You're right,' he said. 'I can see him. He's tormenting me at the moment, but these things will pass. These things will go. Trust me. I need to be the DCI again. I need to be there for the team, strong, so don't tell them.'

Hope walked forward, put her arms around Macleod, and pulled him close. 'Your secret's safe with me,' she said. 'I'm going to help you, Seoras.'

Macleod hugged her back. He thought about how, when they initially had met, he saw her physical beauty. Now he saw her for the person she truly was, his friend, his ally.

'You better let me go. If Jane comes in, she'll be desperately jealous, especially since you've got your hair down.'

'You're not in as the DCI today, you're just visiting. I know you prefer it down. I know you think it makes me look…'

'You can look however you want,' said Macleod.

'How is Jane coping?'

'Jane's doing what she always does,' said Macleod, walking further into the office. 'She's looking after me. She's focusing her attention on me. It scared her. It terrified her. Several times now she's been under threat. That's what makes me think about quitting more than anything else. If it was just me, well, what would I do on my own? You saw me when I was on my own, not a nice man, all caught up in religion and judgment. Not since she came. Not since you came.'

'We never found Norman Greenhalgh's body,' said Hope. 'Are you okay with that?'

'Am I okay with that?' said Macleod, and he almost laughed. 'I don't know what I'm okay with. I go and see this counsellor twice a week. We sit and we talk and I tell him I keep seeing people. I keep saying to him they seem so real and he says, but they're not. How do I feel about what they say to me? There's no justification for what they're saying. It was a mistaken identity.

'And he says that as if it all should be okay, then. That's the worst part of it,' said Macleod. 'I didn't deserve any of this. McNeil did. McNeil should have had this. Then I'm reminded to forgive and forget. That's what they always say, isn't it? Forgive and forget, as if it never happened. How do I say it never happened? How does his wrongdoing get washed away?'

'I thought that was what you believed,' said Hope.

'It is what I believe. I do believe in a new start. I believe in

201

things not being brought up, but how? He delivered a woman to the mainland that had been abused. He betrayed a woman who was destroyed and who then hanged herself in front of a girl, her daughter. She then went on to destroy herself and looked to destroy me. What would have happened if Anna hadn't come through?

'You, Jane, would you have destroyed people? Forgive and forget is the easiest thing to say. It's a cliché. They don't talk about the pain that comes with it.'

There was a rap at the door behind him. 'Come in,' said Hope. Clarissa entered the room and walked slowly over to Macleod, where she took a good look at him.

'What is this? Am I the bull in the cattle market?' he said.

'Well, they wouldn't pay much for you,' said Clarissa, and then she stepped forward and hugged him.

'Thank you,' he whispered in her ear.

'For what?' she said.

'For everything.'

'Well, us oldies have to stick together. In another time and place...' she said.

'I think we'll stop there,' said Macleod. 'You don't want to let Frank hear that.'

'Nor Jane,' she said.

'I think Jane knows, it's only us men that are dumb.'

Clarissa stepped back, almost looking embarrassed that they'd had such a quiet conversation, keeping Hope at bay.

'I guess you both better hear this,' Clarissa said, and walked over, closing the door of the office. 'I came back to save Seoras. Came back because there was unfinished business. It doesn't change the way I felt. I won't be in the team for long. A transfer back to the art team is what I want. To solve crimes that involve beautiful artwork, not the bodies of children and men and women. Don't get me wrong, I love you guys, especially Als out there. You'd better take care of him because he is screwed up at the moment.

'But I'm moving on. And if they can't find me a place in the art team, I am hanging up my shawl and I will go watch my husband cut grass at the local golf club. I may even go back to the clubs.'

'Are you sure about that?' asked Hope. 'Are you sure you want to leave because we could really do with you?'

'She's sure,' said Macleod, 'and she needs to go.'

Hope turned and looked at Macleod, quite shocked. Then she turned back to Clarissa. 'Well, it's your decision. I'm not sure I totally agree with it.'

'It's the best for her,' said Macleod. 'I probably shouldn't have brought you on board. It was just chance that we'd lost Kirsten. I needed somebody with a bit of firepower. Somebody who could handle themself.'

'I know, well aware of that,' said Clarissa. 'I hope I did you proud.'

Macleod walked forward, took her hand and shook it profusely. 'Clarissa, my Rottweiler, thank you. You saved my life.' She nodded and then withdrew from the room.

'Was she embarrassed?' asked Hope.

'You don't really have a problem with feelings towards anyone on the team, do you?' said Macleod. 'Now before you ask, this doesn't go outside of the room.'

'No,' she said, 'I mean, I'm very fond of people.'

'You're fond of me,' said Macleod. 'I'm fond of you. I was a bit more than fond of you at the start. Well, Clarissa is a bit more than fond of me. And on that note, I'll be making my way upstairs. I'll come down and see Ross and everyone later. I need to get back up to this office. Want to take a bit of time. I'll be back shortly but I need to do some acclimatisation.'

'Have they signed you off?'

'Not yet. It'll be soon though. I've got things under control.'

'But not cured.'

'Cure. You say that like I've got a dose of German measles or the cold. Hope, you can't just stick a needle in me and inject me with something. You can't just send me to bed for three weeks to get over this. This is with me for life, I would suspect,' said Macleod. 'Although I hope I can get past it.'

He thought he saw a tear in her eye and as he walked, she whispered quietly and only just within his earshot. 'I am more than fond of you.'

He stopped, turned, gave a bit of a smile and she smiled back. 'Yes, close shave,' he said. 'Worked out for the best.'

Seoras exited the room and something within him felt better for it. In some ways, he'd never really opened up to Hope. She was always kept at that distance. He had a job to do, and any feelings had to go out the window. They were feelings they wouldn't act on anyway, so what was the point? Yet having come so close to death this time, he wondered if it was better to tell things how they were.

Macleod trudged up the stairs, saying hello to a few of the uniformed officers who passed him. He was, after all, well-known in the station. A figurehead in some ways, someone for people to rally around. And, as such, he put on a smiling face, only to a degree, though. They'd have to know he would jump back in quick enough.

As he got to the top of the stairs and walked down the corridor to his office, he saw his secretary sitting outside. She stood up and came over to him. 'Welcome back, Seoras,' she said.

'Thank you, Linda. It's only a brief visit. I hope Jim hasn't messed up my paperwork.'

'He's inside. I think he was trying to tidy up the last before you got in.'

Macleod knocked on the door of his own office, heard 'Enter', and opened the door.

'You don't have to knock for your own office,' said Jim.

'I see you've tidied up.'

'Your paperwork's all up-to-date. I wouldn't do that to you. How much longer do you want me to keep running this? I have my own job to go to.'

Macleod grinned. Jim stood up from behind the desk and came round, shaking Macleod by the hand. 'Good to see you,' he said. 'We nearly lost you.'

'Well, when you've got friends in the places I have,' said Macleod, 'you always know you're going to be all right.'

'Oh,' he said, 'this card came for you.' Jim handed Macleod an envelope which had been opened. 'Apologies,' he said. 'It was addressed to the DCI.'

Macleod pulled the card out, opened it, and saw a very simple picture inside. It was a cross with a sunrise behind it. Inside, a couple of words were handwritten.

A second chance at life. You're welcome.

At the bottom it was signed *Anna*. Jim took his leave and Macleod sat behind his desk. Then he saw him. Just inside the door was a man in a grey habit with a mask. He held a whip in one hand.

'Confess. Mary Smith, who is Mary Smith?' Macleod looked the other way. 'Mary Smith, who is Mary Smith?'

205

'I don't know a Mary Smith,' said Macleod, quietly. 'Mairi. I knew Mairi.'

'Tell me who Mary Smith is.'

The whip was cracked. Macleod flinched, feeling his back spasm. And then he stopped, staring at the door. There was nobody near it. The door opened suddenly with a knock.

'I take it you want coffee, Seoras,' said Linda.

'Very much so,' he said. 'I'd love coffee.'

She smiled and closed the door behind her, and Macleod looked over to see the figure in the grey habit again. He had a long way to go. Such a very long way to go.

Read on to discover the Patrick Smythe series!

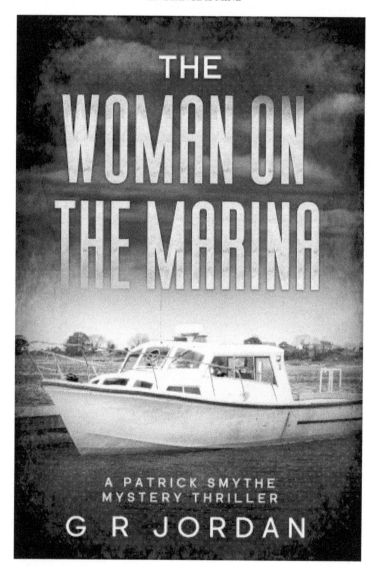

Patrick Smythe is a former Northern Irish policeman who

after suffering an amputation after a bomb blast, takes to the sea between the west coast of Scotland and his homeland to ply his trade as a private investigator. Join Paddy as he tries to work to his own ethics while knowing how to bend the rules he once enforced. Working from his beloved motorboat 'Craigantlet', Paddy decides to rescue a drug mule in this short story from the pen of G R Jordan.

Join G R Jordan's monthly newsletter about forthcoming releases and special writings for his tribe of avid readers and then receive your free Patrick Smythe short story.

Go to https://bit.ly/PatrickSmythe for your Patrick Smythe journey to start!

About the Author

GR Jordan is a self-published author who finally decided at forty that in order to have an enjoyable lifestyle, his creative beast within would have to be unleashed. His books mirror that conflict in life where acts of decency contend with self-promotion, goodness stares in horror at evil, and kindness blindsides us when we at our worst. Corrupting our world with his parade of wondrous and horrific characters, he highlights everyday tensions with fresh eyes whilst taking his methodical, intelligent mainstays on a roller-coaster ride of dilemmas, all the while suffering the banter of their provocative sidekicks.

A graduate of Loughborough University where he masqueraded as a chemical engineer but ultimately played American football, Gary had worked at changing the shape of cereal flakes and pulled a pallet truck for a living. Watching vegetables freeze at -40'C was another career highlight and he was also one of the Scottish Highlands "blind" air traffic controllers.

These days he has graduated to answering a telephone to people in trouble before telephoning other people to sort it out.

Having flirted with most places in the UK, he is now based in the Isle of Lewis in Scotland where his free time is spent between raising a young family with his wife, writing, figuring out how to work a loom and caring for a small flock of chickens. Luckily, his writing is influenced by his varied work and life experience as the chickens have not been the poetical inspiration he had hoped for!

You can connect with me on:
- https://grjordan.com
- https://facebook.com/carpetlessleprechaun

Subscribe to my newsletter:
- https://bit.ly/PatrickSmythe

Also by G R Jordan

G R Jordan writes across multiple genres including crime, dark and action adventure fantasy, feel good fantasy, mystery thriller and horror fantasy. Below is a selection of his work. Whilst all books are available across online stores, signed copies are available at his personal shop.

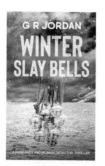 **Winter Slay Bells (Highlands & Islands Detective Book #29)**
https://grjordan.com/product/winter-slay-bells
Sleigh bells ringing send a deadly warning. Christmas shopping becomes a matter of life and death. Can Macleod's team find the festive killer before the streets empty of Yuletide revellers?

The Christmas season becomes a season of dread and panic as a killer stalks the Inverness downtown shoppers during the busiest time of year for beleaguered local commerce. As the town prepares for a winter extravaganza Macleod must wheedle out the brutal murderer before the town is locked down and Christmas is cancelled.

Can you hear what I hear....?

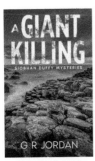

A Giant Killing: Siobhan Duffy Mysteries #1
A body lies on the Giant's boot. Discord, as the master of secrets has been found. Can former spy Siobhan Duffy find the killer before they execute her former colleagues?

When retired operative Siobhan Duffy sees the killing of her former master in the paper, her unease sends her down a path of discovery and fear. Aided by her young housekeeper and scruff of a gardener, Siobhan begins a quest to discover the reason for her spy boss' death and unravels a can of worms today's masters would rather keep closed. But in a world of secrets, the difference between revenge and simple, if brutal, housekeeping becomes the hardest truth to know.

The past is a child who never leaves home!

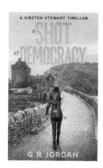

Kirsten Stewart Thrillers

https://grjordan.com/product-category/kirsten-stewart

Join Kirsten Stewart on a shadowy ride through the underbelly of the Highlands of Scotland where among the beauty and splendour of the majestic landscape lies corruption and intrigue to match any city. From murders to extortion, missing children to criminals operating above the law, the Highland former detective must learn a tougher edge to her work as she puts her own life on the line to protect those who cannot defend themselves.

Having left her beloved murder investigation team far behind, Kirsten has to battle personal tragedy and loss while adapting to a whole new way of executing her duties where your mistakes are your own. As Kirsten comes to terms with working with the new team, she often operates as the groups solo field agent, placing herself in danger and trouble to rescue those caught on the dark side of life. With action packed scenes and tense scenarios of murder and greed, the Kirsten Stewart thrillers will have you turning page after page to see your favourite Scottish lass home!

There's life after Macleod, but a whole new world of death!

Jac's Revenge (A Jack Moonshine Thriller #1)

An unexpected hit makes Debbie a widow. The attention of her man's killer spawns a brutal yet classy alter ego. But how far can you play the game before it takes over your life?

All her life, Debbie Parlor lived in her man's shadow, knowing his work was never truly honest. She turned her head from news stories and rumours. But when he was disposed of for his smile to placate a rival crime lord, Jac Moonshine was born. And when Debbie is paid compensation for her loss like her car was written off, Jac decides that enough is enough.

Get on board with this tongue-in-cheek revenge thriller that will make you question how far you would go to avenge a loved one, and how much you would enjoy it!

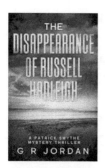

The Disappearance of Russell Hadleigh (Patrick Smythe Book 1)
https://grjordan.com/product/the-disappearance-of-russell-hadleigh
A retired judge fails to meet his golf partner. His wife calls for help while running a fantasy play ring. When Russians start co-opting into a fairly-traded clothing brand, can Paddy untangle the strands before the bodies start littering the golf course?

In his first full novel, Patrick Smythe, the single-armed former policeman, must infiltrate the golfing social scene to discover the fate of his client's husband. Assisted by a young starlet of the greens, Paddy tries to understand just who bears a grudge and who likes to play in the rough, culminating in a high stakes showdown where lives are hanging by the reaction of a moment. If you love pacey action, suspicious motives and devious characters, then Paddy Smythe operates amongst your kind of people.

Love is a matter of taste but money always demands more of its suitor.